BARBARA CARTLAND'S
LIBRARY OF LOVE

No one writes romantic fiction like Barbara Cartland.

Miss Cartland was originally inspired by the best of the romantic novelists she read as a girl—Elinor Glyn, Ethel M. Dell, Ian Hay and E. M. Hull. Convinced that her own wide audience would also delight in her favorite authors, Barbara Cartland has taken their classic tales of romance and specially adapted them for today's readers.

BARBARA CARTLAND'S LIBRARY OF LOVE

Barbara Cartland's Library of Love

THE GREAT MOMENT
BY ELINOR GLYN

CONDENSED BY
BARBARA CARTLAND

DUCKWORTH

Casebound edition first published 1980 by
Gerald Duckworth & Co Ltd
The Old Piano Factory
43 Gloucester Crescent
London NW1

ISBN 0 7156 1474 6

Glyn, Elinor
    The great moment. – (Barbara Cartland's
library of love).
    I. Title   II. Cartland, Barbara   III. Series
823'.9'1F   PR6013.L8G/

ISBN 0–7156–1474–6

Printed in Great Britain by
Billing & Sons Limited
Guildford, London and Worcester

Introduction
by
Barbara Cartland

This is the first time that Elinor Glyn had an American hero in one of her novels, and how wildly attractive he is! After I read *The Great Moment* in 1923 I longed to meet an American like Bayard Delaval.

Nadine, the heroine, whose mother was a Russian gipsy, is wild, passionate, unpredictable, but beautiful and pure. The two grip the imagination and leave one breathless until the last page.

Chapter One

He could not understand a word she was saying as she came nearer and nearer to him, calling out something in Russian each time she passed in the wild dance among the other gipsies.

A fierce creature, sinuous and passionate, with red lips and strange blue eyes. Blue eyes in that dark face!

Sir Edward Pelham, tenth of his line, a reserved, conventional Englishman of forty-one years, felt his blood run as never before in his life.

Everyone was a little drunk by now. It was three o'clock in the morning, the Prince's party had not begun until midnight, and all Saint Petersburg knew that these orgies did not end until dawn.

The gipsy troop had been dancing for an hour and a kind of madness seemed to be seizing everyone. The face of the Madonna in the ikon gently smiled, as in pity at human failings.

But now the chief of the troop called a halt, and the obedient girls drew back into line.

Only Nada, the lovely, wicked, unbiddable Nada, was determined to go on, and when the

1

chief seized her roughly to pull her back, she turned upon him and bit his arm!

With a cry of rage the man wiped off the blood with his sleeve, and would have beaten her, but the Englishman rushed forward and took her from him.

Then with the spring of a panther she was on the table, and, sweeping the glasses and dishes aside, she began to dance madly.

The musicians, exalted to frenzy, never had played so well, and amidst a scene of indescribable excitement and intoxication, at last the beautiful, wild thing fell back, exhausted, into Sir Edward's arms.

❊ ❊ ❊

And the memory of her kisses stayed with him still.

❊ ❊ ❊

Out there in the chill November sunlight he could see his daughter, Nadine. How like Nada she was growing—what was to be done?

❊ ❊ ❊

Miss Blenkensop walked on a little ahead. Nadine was in one of her impossible moods, and it was best to leave the child to herself.

She had stopped for a moment to speak to one of the gardeners, old Prodgers, who was sweeping the dead leaves from the lawn.

Hester Blenkensop's life at Pelham Court could not be considered a bed of roses, in spite of the liberal salary she received and the complete authority she exercised.

The truth was that her charge, Nadine Pelham, had a temperament ill-suited to the conventional standards of this admirable governess!

2

Miss Blenkensop could never be quite certain what she meant to do next, or how any fresh aspect of even the most ordinary branch of knowledge she was trying to drum into her head was going to affect her!

But Sir Edward trusted her completely, and she was not a woman to betray a trust.

So she stayed on year after year, buried away there down in the country, miles from anywhere, in a secluded corner of Somerset, far from the world.

Nadine's conversation with Prodgers didn't last for very long, for they were going into the chapel across the lawn to put the wreath on Nada's tomb, a duty performed every Saturday, summer and winter.

But today the wreath was a particularly nice one, for tomorrow would be the tenth anniversary of the death of the beautiful gipsy.

Nadine knew every bit of the carving upon the tomb, fine marble in excellent taste, and ever since she could think she had wondered what her mother was like, who slept inside it.

Meanwhile, in the library, Sir Edward was musing. He owed an obvious duty to the child. He must do everything he possibly could to crush out that unfortunate wildness in her which Blenkensop's report showed every time he returned home.

To surround her with the quietest influences, to keep her away from the world, no one could be better than Blenkensop, and the French maid, Augustine, had the highest references.

But with the instincts she would be bound to inherit, as well as the beauty, of her mother, the

3

most careful training would be necessary to eliminate the Russian gipsy instincts, and to shape her into the Pelham mould.

Sir Edward looked up to the portrait above the mantelpiece of an ancestor of his of Elizabeth's time. They had come down in an unbroken line—always respected, always admirable members of their rank and family.

And now an accident had robbed him of his dead brother's son, a promising boy—and the whole thing would go to a distant cousin, Eustace by name—one whom he had never seen.

Oh, what a tragedy that he himself had no son. And yet, nothing bad was known of Eustace, he was a worthy young man just entering the diplomatic service.

And if Nadine had been a boy? Who knows? And here Sir Edward sighed.

* * *

Music had a powerful effect upon Nadine, especially certain kinds.

Sir Edward had a party to shoot in his large coverts early in December 1913, and among them was an attaché from the Russian Embassy, Prince Kurousov—a rather decadent wit, with a pretty talent for the violin.

Nadine, who came down in the afternoon for tea with Blenkie, took a violent fancy to him; she sat as close to him as she could, and gazed up into his face, and when he began playing Russian music in the crimson drawing-room after tea, it seemed to Sir Edward that the spirit of Nada lived again in their child.

Prince Kurousov played the "Red Sarafane,"

and he remembered that this was the very air which the gipsies had played to please the Grand Duke, and which Nada had danced to, on that unforgettable night when she had first melted into his arms.

Nadine jumped up from her seat beside Miss Blenkensop, and, picking up her skirts, began to pirouette about the room, all sense of shyness or decorum quite forgotten in her pleasure.

The guests were delighted and full of admiration. Only Lord Crombie looked on with a glass fixed in his knowing old eye, and Sir Edward winced with the pain of his memories.

"You'll probably have to be careful with that child, Ned," Lord Crombie said. "Watch her movements, she has not learned those from her dancing mistress!"

Nadine's shoulders were fluttering in a rhythmic fashion. Watching her, a wild delight came over Prince Kurousov.

"Beautiful little Russian gipsy!" he said, throwing down his violin and picking her up in his arms.

But Nadine turned upon him with a fierce gesture, and showed all her strong white teeth. If he had not let her go that instant she would have bitten his arm.

A great anger came over Sir Edward, anger and fear, and he advanced towards the child with a look in his grey eyes which seemed to freeze the blood in her veins.

Before he could speak to her, Lord Crombie linked his arm in Sir Edward's and drew him towards the group of men by the fireplace, while Lady Crombie stretched out her hands to the

5

frightened creature, and drew her to her side, telling her lightly how charmingly she had danced.

Nadine pulled herself together, the years of stern rule and discipline reasserted their influence, and she sank upon the sofa beside this kind friend, trembling all over but bravely keeping back her tears.

"Papa . . . did not think I danced . . . well," she whispered, with a sob in her rather deep voice, which always had a husky note in it. "He was very angry . . . oh! dear Lady Crombie . . . why?"

"I think you imagined it, darling; we all admired you so much."

Lady Crombie took the little olive-ivory face in her hands and looked kindly into the blue eyes.

"Are you lonely, dear little girl, here in this great house, with no one to play with but your dogs?"

The tears welled up slowly now, and then brimmed over.

I don't know, I suppose I am . . . but I wouldn't be if everything I wanted to do was not wrong."

Some of the other guests came up then and joined them, and Lady Crombie could say no more; but when her husband came into her dressing-room as she was resting before dinner, she said to him:

"I think Ned is making a terrible mistake in the way he is suppressing that child; she wants love, kindness, and understanding, not Miss Blenkensop all the time."

Lord Crombie warmed his back at the fire. He was a whimsical old bird, and nothing much escaped him.

"There are two methods of dealing with savages: you beat them into submission, and they think you are a god; or you arouse their devotion, and they serve you as a slave.

"Nadine is half-savage, you know, and Ned has not the kind of nature to call forth much devotion, dear old pal that he is."

"I am glad you said *half*-savage," Lady Crombie retorted indignantly. "She is the sweetest, most tender-hearted little creature, and anything could be got out of her by sympathy and love.

"But they will drive her to wickedness before she is grown up, unless they crush the life and spirit out of her."

"Ned has some pretty terrible memories of her mother, you know; nothing would tame her, she disgraced him at every moment, but he adored her to the end."

"The more reason, then, that he should try to understand her child."

"Well, I'll give him a hint how the matter has struck you, Viola. Meanwhile, you'd better dress, or you will be late."

But that night Nadine cried herself to sleep, and in her uneasy dreams she could always hear the "Red Sarafane."

*　　*　　*

The war produced very few changes at Pelham Court.

Sir Edward returned to the Foreign Office, which he had retired from years before, and was often away on distant missions.

Miss Blenkensop worked at war comforts incessantly, and Nadine also. But Nadine hated sewing; she always longed to be a soldier and go out and fight!

Nadine at the age of eighteen, when Sir Edward returned in 1920 from Japan, was a girl well polished in literature and the polite sciences; but of the world and of life she was as absolutely ignorant as she had been at age ten.

The first night that she and her father dined together, Blenkie had a headache and was in bed—fortunately, Sir Edward felt, as he was able to study his child uninterruptedly during the meal.

She had grown into a beautiful young woman, with a fascination about her not easy to define.

Was it her over-voluptuous mouth? Or the strange contrast of her bright blue eyes with that ivory-olive skin?

She was still slender and childish-looking in figure, but somehow, nothing of the child seemed to be left in her eyes.

They were mysterious and passionate, and made people feel uneasy when they looked at them deeply.

"Papa, I am sick to death of Pelham Court. I loathe the country. I want now to go out and sample the world."

"We must see about it, Nadine."

"Which means you don't intend to take me!"

A rebellious light came into her eyes, although she still stood in absolute awe of her father, just as her mother had done.

There was something in the cold, cynical regard of Sir Edward which froze most people, and which dominated completely that savage half in Nadine.

It was that part of her spirit that she had inherited from him which alone was able to stand against him, but that was not sufficiently developed yet to show!

As she spoke, there came to her father the old feeling of fear—what would it mean when once she knew the world?

Marriage was the best thing which could happen to her; fortunately, a very suitable one could be arranged.

Eustace Pelham was at home, on leave from Rome, and if only the two young people could be brought together before Nadine had seen a choice of partners, the desire of Sir Edward's heart might be accomplished, and the family could go on through his daughter and his cousin's son.

He would write to the Crombies, who were coming down next week for a farewell visit before they left for Washington, and ask them to bring Eustace with them.

Sir Edward's eye then travelled to Nadine's simple dress. Yes, she would look very different in some pretty Paris clothes.

Lady Crombie, who knew all about these sorts of things, could be asked to bring some, as she was in Paris at the moment.

Meanwhile, Nadine was wondering what the return of her father would mean.

The years of war had seemed so long to her, buried in the country, and he had come home so seldom!

Of course he could not help that, poor Papa, he had to do his duty; but now the war was over, and surely in the coming season he would take her up to London and let her enjoy life!

There was one book which Nadine loved: it was the story of the knight, Bayard, *sans peur et sans reproche.*

Miss Blenkensop, while completely discouraging even the simplest novels, had had sense enough to see that such a nature as Nadine's must have some hero to worship, and when a beautifully illustrated copy of this admirable gentleman's adventures came down among the birthday gifts for her pupil's fourteenth birthday, Miss Blenkensop was delighted to encourage interest in it.

In fact she looked upon the book as sent from heaven, for here was a romantic history absolutely devoid of any allusion to sex. Here was a knight whose love for the Lady of Frussasco could be dwelt on, and the beauty of it extolled.

And in short, Bayard had been made to stand as a type of perfect man, and in Nadine's pure wild heart he became enshrined as king.

She had built her own romance round him as she grew older, and now Bayard, for her, represented the lover who would come and set her free, who would take her far away from Blenkie and Papa and Pelham Court, out to see the world.

But the good knight would certainly not have recognized the picture her imagination had made of him, could he have returned to earth!

When she thought of the future, it was invariably of some romantic meeting with her hero; and in some modern way she felt that she too would give a broidered sleeve to spur him on to victory!

Perhaps he would be a politician, perhaps a soldier; but whoever he might be, she meant to be his star!

The book itself, with its beautiful binding, had become a sort of talisman; she had it always on her table near her, although now she seldom opened its leaves, and the real story of the knight interested her no more.

❀   ❀   ❀

On the day, a fortnight later, when the Crombies and Eustace Pelham were expected, Nadine was having a wild gallop through the park.

Old James, the groom who had accompanied her when on horseback since her childhood, found it difficult to keep up with her.

The very fact of the Crombies arriving was a pleasure to Nadine, although she had heard nothing of Eustace. Anyone from the outside world made a change, and two of the dresses had come from Paris, and that was also a joy.

But there was always Blenkie, watchful and restraining, and it was only when out with old James that Nadine ever got away from her.

She might not hunt, that too was forbidden, but she could gallop to her heart's content along Forwood Gorse and the West Down, with James behind her.

Sir Edward was sitting alone in the library, that lofty, oak-panelled room with its many books, and things were shaping themselves.

Lady Crombie had written that Eustace Pelham had taken kindly to the idea of an alliance with the daughter of the head of the family.

He was of the opinion that it would be a good plan to keep fortune and property together, and he would ask Nadine to become his wife on the first suitable moment during his visit.

11

Lady Crombie wrote:

There is no romance about Eustace, Ned. (You will say, of course, that that is a fortunate thing!) He has seen too much of the world to retain any illusions, and he shares your views that marriage turns out more happily if based upon material suitability.

You will be answerable for Nadine. I can only tell you, my dear old friend, that I am glad that is not my part of the business, for perhaps Nadine will not like him at all, and upset the whole apple cart.

When Sir Edward read this part of the letter he frowned a little, then put it aside, on top of one that had come that morning from America.

It had interested him, since Nada died, to dabble a little in mines all over the world, and he had already acquired a cool million or two out of the Gold Stamp Mining Corporation in Nevada, which he owned jointly with one Elihu Bronson—an American millionaire.

Bronson had written to say that the head mining engineer would come in, on his way to catch the boat at Southampton, with the latest particulars. He had been in England on business.

What a bore! The fellow might be turning up today.

Then when these two letters were safely in one drawer, another was unlocked, and Sir Edward drew out a jewel case which he had but yesterday got from the safe.

He opened it, and his whole cynical face changed; back came the vision of Nada the Gipsy,

12

and that wonderful night! How she had maddened his every sense, and *how* he had loved her!

And what pleasure it had been to give her these jewels on their way through Paris, sapphires and diamonds as blue and as bright as her eyes.

And now they should all be Nadine's—upon her wedding day.

As he held up a necklace, he half-murmured a prayer to the spirit of Nada, to help him to guide the destiny of their child, who was growing so like, too like, her mother.

Then, angry with himself, he got up and rang the bell.

Nadine ran up the steps after her ride and went into the great hall. She was singing a merry tune; off went her hat and onto the music stool, and the gloves followed.

"Sir Edward wishes to see you in the library, Miss," said Mumford, the portly butler, as Nadine ran past him.

She had known and dreaded these summons to the library all her life, and Mumford knew it and sympathized with her secretly.

Nadine reached her father's side, and was told to sit down. Her heart beat a little faster; he was so quiet, it was evidently something perfectly awful that she had done.

Sir Edward felt nervous—how was he to begin?

The jewels were something to start from, so he opened the case, and Nadine's eyes brightened with interest.

"These were your mother's jewels, dear child," he said, "and they are all to be yours on your wedding day."

He paused. The female delight in baubles was overcoming Nadine: all primitive things affected her at this stage of her evolution.

She had taken in that the jewels were to be hers. She took them out and touched them tenderly then she held a pendant up against her dark habit, and caressed a great pearl which hung from it.

Her father was talking again, and he was not scolding her. What was he saying?

Wedding day! Her cousin, Eustace Pelham ... coming to ask her to be his wife ...

She dropped the necklace and clasped her hands. Bayard at last! Coming to set her free! Oh, how altogether divine!

She bounded from the chair that she had drawn up meekly to her father's side, and hugged him.

"Oh, you darling pet! What's he like ... Eustace? When shall I see him? Oh, Papa!"

"In a half-hour from now, Nadine, so run along and dress. You must do justice to being my daughter and the mistress of this house."

She tore through the hall, singing at the top of her voice, and on the stairs met Miss Blenkensop coming down.

Her hard face expressed her disapproval of so much exuberance, but she allowed herself to be pulled along into Nadine's room.

It was a pleasant room, with its old English chintzes and its simple Chippendale furniture. Pictures of the cats and dogs the owner loved were about, a photograph of Sir Edward adorned the dressing-table, an ivory-bound Prayer Book lay on the table by the bed, and on another table drawn up to the sofa was the *Story of Bayard*, the perfect knight.

Winnie, an elderly black-and-tan terrier, had been sleeping beside the fireplace in her basket, but she got up to greet her mistress.

Nadine let go of Blenkie and seized her precious book. The belief had come true . . . a real Bayard was arriving this very afternoon.

She dropped the volume again, after having clasped it ecstatically to her heart, and was now caressing Winnie and telling of her joy.

Miss Blenkensop picked up the book; she greatly disapproved of these outbursts, so theatrical, so un-English, and not quite in good taste; but when her eye caught the *Story of Bayard*, she felt relieved.

That kind of love was just as it should be, so she retired from the room rather reassured. And Nadine, left to herself, told everything to Winnie.

"Bayard, my knight . . . coming at last to set me free, Winnie. But his name's not Bayard . . . it's Eustace."

She wrinkled her nose.

"E-U-S-T-A-C-E. . . . Do I like the name 'Eustace'? Not much. Sounds awfully good, Winnie, not like you and me. But what's in a name, my black beauty? We can call him 'Bayard' if we wish."

Suddenly she heard a car arrive, and in frantic excitement she rushed to the window. Could it be . . . was it . . . ?

Someone was getting out of a taxi, a man, a young man. Her heart beat very fast. He was a

15

tallish person, clean-cut, and slim-waisted. He was clean-shaven too, and somehow his clothes did not look quite English.

He glanced up at the house after he had given directions to the taxi man, and Nadine could see that he had a strong, quiet face, and that his eyes were grey.

He looked like a gentleman ... and ... yes ... he could very well be her knight. All the suppressed, unconscious, passionate desires of her half-savage nature arose suddenly.

Oh, how divine to have a lover, and this one, tall and slim and strong! Nadine's heroes were not those whom she could rule.

A hero must adore her, and do anything she pleased, of course; but if he chose, he must be able to make her obey him.

He must have something of the lion-tamer about him as well as tenderness!

That he should be clever was a secondary consideration. He must be a ruler, and warmly fond.

The man below at the door now bent to pat the two sheep-dogs, who had come out to sample the newcomer.

"He likes dogs," commented Nadine.

Then he disappeared into the house with the footman who had come to the door, and she turned excitedly to Winnie once more.

"He's a darling, Winnie, and I shall love him, I know."

Then she rang the bell excitedly, and when her maid came, she gave orders to see both her new frocks; and while Augustine went to fetch them, she literally tore off her habit, and danced about the room, wrapping herself in a pink satin dressing-gown.

Yes, the pale grey frock was a triumph of simplicity, and nice and short; she would put that on.

Then when presently Augustine brought shoes and stockings for her to put on, she kicked the little pink-satin mules, which she had thrust her toes into, right up to the ceiling, and one fell on the maid's head.

"Tiens, Mademoiselle!" protested Augustine, highly irritated; but Nadine was blissfully indifferent.

Then her hair had to be specially arranged; something told her she must not annoy her father in any way, and, finally getting the maid out of the room for a moment, she searched for, and found, a tiny box of face powder which she had concealed in the strapping of the cushion of a chair.

With Winnie watching her sympathetically, she carefully rubbed her face with the minute puff.

This powder was a delightful secret. She had bought it one day at the chemist's in Yeominster, when Blenkie's back was turned, and the little box appealed to her fancy.

She had never put it on before to go downstairs, but surely when one was going to meet one's future husband, one had every right to make oneself look as beautiful as possible!

Her skin, pure and fine as ivory, with its olive tinge, was velvety enough without any adornment. And finally, very pleased with herself but a little nervous, she started to go to the library, where tea would soon be coming, and all the guests arrived.

Meanwhile, the young man who had come in the taxi presented a longish envelope and was asked to wait a moment by the big fireplace in the great hall, while the letter was taken to the master of the house in the library.

Sir Edward was still sitting in his chair, gazing in front of him, as when Nadine had left him a few moments before.

He read the missive quietly. It was from his partner, Elihu Bronson, and introduced Mr. Bayard Delaval, head mining engineer of the Gold Stamp Mining Corporation, who, the writer said, was a Harvard man, one of the younger Delavals of Washington, and one of the cleverest mining experts out West.

He would explain how necessary it was that Sir Edward should come out to America this spring, and take a trip out to Gold Stamp to see for himself how things were progressing.

"Ask Mr. Delaval to come in, Mumford," Sir Edward said.

And in a moment Bayard Delaval made his entrance. He had been taking in things while he waited. It must mean a great deal, this old house with its accumulation of associations covering hundreds of years.

How much tradition must mean as a principle of action! How would he feel if these were his ancestors looking down at him from the walls?

Delaval was quite as old a name as Pelham; they had come from Northamptonshire to Virginia about two hundred years ago.

He must look the history up someday, when he had time; his father had always made such a study of it, and he had had a kind of feeling that he must be worthy of it.

A man's spirit and his will to do mattered more than any ancestors in the world though, he decided, and then followed Mumford into Sir Edward's presence.

Sir Edward greeted Mr. Delaval cordially, and they talked for a little, keeping strictly to business. Then, warming to the young man, he said:

"Do let me persuade you to stop over the weekend."

It was a real temptation to Bayard Delaval. He had never seen a great English house before; it was his first visit to Europe, and novelty interested him.

A keen psychologist, he was accustomed to analyze the meaning of things, and realized that these old families, with their hereditary points of view, were worth studying.

He was sorry to say, though, that he could not stay. He must catch the *Mauretania* at Southampton; but they would meet again out West, in Nevada, he hoped, very shortly.

When he had gone, Sir Edward mused to himself that the fellow had charm, and his not staying might be just as well.

Then the Crombies arrived, and Eustace Pelham.

Diplomacy seems to stamp people more strongly than any other profession. No one could mistake Lord Crombie for anything but an old diplomat, or Eustace Pelham for anything but a young one.

"Quite one of the family, but a trifle overbred," Sir Edward thought, as he looked at his

19

heir. "It won't hurt our descendants to have Nadine's half-plebian blood balancing things."

Eustace was groomed to perfection, and had an indifferent, aloof manner; the social duties of a diplomatic career had never been neglected by him.

He was the adored of cosmopolitan female society in the different capitals he had already been appointed to.

He liked exotic women and never spoke to girls. But one must marry sometime, and it was better to have a wife with a fortune than otherwise.

His cousin Nadine was too young ever to hamper his freedom in any way, and not too much would be expected of him.

He had brought a diamond engagement ring down with him, and meant to go through with the thing as arranged.

"Beastly nuisance, of course," he decided, "but then any tie is a nuisance."

They were already in the library when Nadine came slowly down the stairs.

Her heart was beating so fast that she felt she could hardly be sure of controlling her voice. She paused a moment at the library door, then went in.

She hardly dared to look up at the tall figure which stood beyond her father, and eagerly greeted Lady Crombie near the door.

"How you have grown, dear," her old friend said, as she kissed her. "And how attractive you have become," she added to herself.

Then Lord Crombie gave his greetings, and finally Sir Edward drew the man behind him forward, and Nadine raised her blue eyes and looked

at him, and over her face there came a blank
stare. . . .

This . . . this could not be . . . Eustace? Eustace
whom she had seen out her window, arriving.
Eustace . . . who was to be Bayard . . . her knight!

She could have cried in her disappointment.
This namby-pamby man! She became suddenly
very pale, and she hardly heard her father's voice
saying:

"This is your cousin Eustace, Nadine, dear
child. You have never met before, but I want you
to be very good friends."

Then she felt a nerveless, indifferent hand take
her cold little fingers, but she could not force herself to speak a word.

Old Lord Crombie put his eyeglass in his eye
and observed things.

"Ned has got a stiff proposition to put forward
there," he silently reflected sagely.

And then the servants brought in the tea, and
everyone talked at once, and Nadine's silence
passed unnoticed.

But when she reached her room again and
called Winnie from her basket, she burst into passionate tears.

Chapter
Two

Who was the man she had seen out the window?

Why did no one speak of an arrival?

These thoughts troubled Nadine the next day.

Visitors were of rare enough occurrence. And such a visitor! How had he come and gone and no one commented upon it?

She would have to ask her father.

But Sir Edward was in one of his unapproachable moods, when it was impossible to say anything to him that he did not want to hear.

So, driven to desperation, Nadine spoke to Blenkie.

"Did you know someone came yesterday when I was dressing to go down to tea, Blenkie ... a gentleman ... who was he?"

"I heard of no one, Nadine."

How could she find out? She could of course ask Mumford. As he passed her in the hall she put her question:

"Who was it who arrived by the side door yesterday afternoon in a taxi from the West Lodge, Mumford?"

"He was from Sir Edward's American mine, Miss, on business."

"Are you sure, Mumford? I thought it was a gentleman." Nadine's voice was full of disappointment.

'They do tell me, Miss, that everyone is the same there; but I did not stand no nonsense of that sort from my nephew when he came back last year. If a man works in mines, he is a miner, and there is no more to it, Miss."

Nadine went on her way.

So he was only a miner, her Knight Bayard! Oh, what a terrible pity!

Her mind still affected by the charm of her supposed knight, she had found her cousin a hideous disillusion at dinner the evening before; and afterwards, in the drawing-room, she could see nothing but his faults.

Lady Crombie felt very uncertain as to the wisdom of the course that they were all taking, but she never gave unasked-for advice, and having promised her old friend that she would help him, she meant to keep her word.

And so a week went by, and the outstanding conviction which settled down into the brain of Nadine was that resistance was hopeless: it was either Eustace and the world, or Blenkie and Pelham Court forever.

She had moments when she was like a fierce, caged animal, but just as the wild beast knows and obeys its keeper, so she put up no fight with her father.

Then some other part of her nature came uppermost, and suggested to her that freedom was worth any price she might be asked to pay for it, even the meek acceptance of Eustace as a husband.

But the Pan-spirit in her could not resist playing pranks, and she was infinitely irritating to Eustace.

She made obvious jokes, she was capricious, and she raced her horse always ahead of his when they rode together.

She lagged behind when they walked, she clung to Lady Crombie's skirts whenever there seemed to be a prospect of being alone with him, and when he was not exasperated he was bored to death.

Nadine's was not the type which drew him; the fascinations which would have driven another man crazy left Eustace Pelham completely cold.

He thought her a silly, excitable tomboy, and felt an amount of self-pity that he should have to take such a wife.

But he had come there prepared to ask her to marry him, and did not mean to be turned aside from his purpose; for, after all, marriage was a shackle and no pleasure, however you looked at it.

"Of course when she sees how absurd she is, among the delightful, civilized people in Rome, she will change," he reflected, as he stroked his little moustache, or settled his immaculate white tie.

But he could not always hide his boredom with her.

Then Nadine became piqued. Even to her perceptions, which were not the keenest, it was evident that Eustace was unattracted.

She, the woman, meant nothing to him. He was only going to marry her because she was her father's daughter, and once more the overpowering influence of Sir Edward seemed to crush her.

Then, some dormant sense of desire for conquest was aroused in her: she must get away from being a nonentity.

Why could she not make this man feel? Perhaps he was just as wooden as he looked, or was it something wanting in herself?

She was very quiet that day when she thought of these things. Sir Edward was growing anxious.

Lady Crombie had been asked to inform Miss Blenkensop in regard to the affair, and the two ladies talked things over.

Blenkie was of the opinion that Mr. Pelham had better get his proposal made as soon as possible.

"If Nadine once *determined* she won't accept him, there would be no use in going on; he had better clinch the matter while she is still undecided."

Lady Crombie agreed with her, and felt that she herself ought to make the opportunity, that very night after dinner.

Blenkie spoke to Nadine before dinner, when she came into her room and found her pupil putting on a fresh new frock from Paris.

"What a charming young man Mr. Pelham is, Nadine," she said. "He is so refined and gentleman-like, it is a pleasure to be in his company."

"I am glad you think so," snapped Nadine. "I hate everything about him. I want to rumple his hair, untie his ties, upset my soup plate over his splendidly creased trousers; but I am going to marry him all right. Never fear, Blenkie."

"Nadine!" was all Miss Blenkensop could

utter, and then she walked in grim dignity from the room.

At dinner Miss Pelham behaved as Miss Pelham should. She was sweet and not jerky, and she talked nicely to Eustace, saying how much she longed to visit Rome and study its antiquities.

Lady Crombie and Sir Edward exchanged glances: the moment seemed propitious.

Eustace must be given a hint to propose to her that evening, if the idea did not seem to be presenting itself naturally. Only Lord Crombie had a whimsical smile in his old eyes.

Nadine sat down at the piano and began idly touching the keys. Sir Edward and Lord Crombie came through the hall and went into the library.

Eustace felt he had better get it over! He had been carrying the engagement ring in his pocket continuously since his arrival.

Nadine knew it was coming, this only key to freedom! So she controlled herself as well as she could, and when she had finished a fox-trot that she was playing, she twisted round upon the music seat and faced him, as he reclined in the most comfortable arm-chair.

He settled his collar for a minute, and then he began:

"It was awfully nice of Sir Edward arranging this marriage for us, Nadine, wasn't it? I'll be a very lucky fellow if you'll take me."

He hardly glanced at her while he took the engagement-ring case from his waistcoat pocket and began removing the ring, a big diamond one, from its white velvet bed.

Nadine did not speak; she nodded her head.

Her heart seemed very still. It was all so terribly matter-of-fact, this, the turning point in her life!

In a supercilious, indifferent way, Eustace took one of her hands, which were loosely clasped in her lap—it happened to be the right one—and began putting the ring upon the third finger.

Nadine realized the mistake and its implication of his indifference, and she drew back a little indignantly.

"By Jove! I was putting it on the wrong hand," Eustace exclaimed, laughing rather fatuously. "How stupid of me!"

"Yes." And she gave him her left one.

She felt frozen, and, rather laboriously, Eustace placed the diamond upon the engagement-ring finger and kissed her hand coldly.

Then he subsided complacently back into his chair and flicked a scrap of fluff from his sleeve with his over-bred, delicate fingers.

A wild resentment filled Nadine.

Was this the way proposals were made in that aristocratic Pelham world to which she had the misfortune to belong?

And then a vision came of the face of the man who had looked up at her from the side door! Oh, what a pity, pity, pity, that he wasn't Eustace!

Nadine looked at him furiously, then bounded up from her seat and walked quickly towards the library, leaving him, surprised and disconcerted, to follow more slowly.

Sir Edward and Lord Crombie were talking together, as they warmed their backs by the blazing logs, and they looked up expectantly as the excited little figure burst into the room, and Nadine came forward and took her father's arm, hiding a flushed face against his coat.

Then Sir Edward noticed the ring, and taking her hand showed it to his old friend with a triumphant and benevolent smile.

Eustace had reached them by this time, and there were congratulations all round.

But as they went off to bed later on, Lord Crombie remarked:

"You are taking chances, Ned. The days are late for the disposal of daughters willy-nilly. This is only the first act of the comedy, my dear boy."

Sir Edward frowned.

* * *

Oh, the weary days that followed! The Crombies had to leave on the next Saturday, and the fiancés, but for the watchful eyes of Blenkie, would be often alone.

Nadine used to get away after breakfast as soon as possible, on one pretext or another, and then she would ride with Eustace just before lunch.

He had not had the slightest desire to kiss her. He felt it would be like kissing some tiresome little boy; a peck at her hand in a ceremonious way, as they said good-night, was as far as he had ventured.

He would have to be a little more lover-like, he supposed, but how she had got on his nerves! Every giggle, and Nadine sometimes giggled from sheer nervousness, made him wince.

She wondered and wondered what life would be like with him when they were married and went off to Rome. He would begin making some kind of love to her, she supposed.

29

What would it be like? She was too innocent to make any mental pictures.

Her imagination got so far as Eustace taking her into his arms and kissing her, and there came a thrill, but it was always because Eustace's face had changed into that of the stranger at the side door.

She was really answering to the romantic springtime thoughts of her nature, and Eustace was only a peg upon whom she hung them.

After the thrill had passed, and she realized that it was Eustace who would one day caress her, and not her dream knight, then a blank horrible deadness settled upon her, and she would be silent for hours.

A fortnight went by, and the strain began to tell upon Nadine's physical health.

And the old family doctor, who had come up to Pelham Court to see an ailing housemaid, was struck by her appearance when they met on the stairs.

He was perhaps the only person who really apprehended the nature of Nadine, or had any sympathy for her.

He paused and had a chat, and then he went into the library to see Sir Edward.

He spoke his mind quite freely. The girl wanted a change. Take her away somewhere and let her have some different air and new interests.

Sir Edward was most concerned. He had intended that the wedding should take place soon after Whitsuntide, he said, and they would be going over to Paris to get the trousseau next week.

But old Dr. Wilson shook his head.

"Do not marry her off just yet, I pray of you, Sir Edward. Why not take her for a trip round the world first?"

Sir Edward looked the doctor straight in the eyes.

"I have got to go to America on business, to inspect a mine I have out there in Nevada. I had intended to start after the wedding; you would advise, perhaps, that I go sooner, and take my daughter and her fiancé with me?"

Dr. Wilson thought this an excellent idea, and the sooner they could get off the better. So that evening at dinner Sir Edward made known his decision.

Nadine could not suppress her joy.

"Oh, Papa, you darling! Oh, how perfectly divine!" And she rushed from her chair and kissed him.

Sir Edward thrilled a little in spite of himself. It was all so like Nada when she was pleased about something, but it was too unconventional for the Pelham standard.

This American trip suited Eustace admirably. He had three months' leave from his diplomatic duties, and the charming and sophisticated American ladies he had met in various capitals of Europe would welcome him, he knew.

He was in no hurry for the wedding to take place!

So, by the beginning of June, this highly respectable English family found themselves on board a great liner, with their pompous personal servants, and Blenkie, and heaven knows how many English leather trunks and bags, along with them!

And for the first time in her life Nadine Pelham felt free.

Free to rise early, before Blenkie was awake, who shared the large state-room of their suite with her, and race round the upper boat deck with some children who played there.

Free to make a noise with them. Free to pretend that she was sleepy in the afternoon and lie with half-closed blue eyes and dream.

The band on board played Russian music in the restaurant, and it seemed to awaken something fierce in Nadine.

Her nostrils began to quiver and her feet unconsciously marked time as they tapped the floor.

At the next table a couple of men sat alone; one was the typical friend of the very rich, and the other was a millionaire by the name of Howard B. Hopper.

Howard B. Hopper believed in money, it had always been able to buy him what he wanted in life, and Nadine Pelham attracted him extremely.

Her exotic type showing through the breeding she had inherited from her father made a rare combination, he thought. That was the kind of wife he meant to throw the handkerchief to presently.

He meant to take a first place in European society also!

He gave his orders to Terry Potter.

"I want to become acquainted with that little cutie over there, Terry. I've had my eye *on* her since the ship left. The head steward tells me her father's *some* swell, and they've never been to God's country before.

"They're on their way to California now, but

I want to sample the brand before they leave New York. . . ."

But for once the gods were not on the side of the millionaire. No machinations of the astute Terry could secure an introduction.

Eustace was taking a rest cure, and slept most of each day in his state-room, and it would have taken the pluck and assurance of a toy Pekinese to endeavour to scrape acquaintance with Sir Edward!

So Mr. Howard B. Hopper could only stare from afar during the rest of the voyage, and vent his annoyance upon the discomfitted friend of the very rich.

"There is an impossible bounder, Miss Blenkensop, sitting at the next table to us in the restaurant, who looks at Nadine. See that she is never unattended." Those were Sir Edward's orders to Blenkie.

So for the last three days of the voyage the feeling of freedom which Nadine had been revelling in began to lessen, and by the time they reached New York the old sense of being a prisoner had settled down upon her again.

Her father and Eustace stood on each side of her as they all watched the entrance to New York harbour.

Nadine's excitement was intense. She was going to land in a new country, where, she had heard, girls did as they pleased.

Mr. Bronson and his daughter, Sadie, were on the dock to meet them, and Nadine was enchanted at the thought of meeting someone young and of this free nation.

There was very little Sadie Bronson did not know about life, except how to make it satisfy her. Everything she had wanted her father had given her, until now.

But one of her friends in California had married a French marquis of undoubted position and prestige, and Sadie felt that she must marry a European aristocrat also.

Eustace's type pleased her; there could be no mistake as to what breed he belonged to, and as Sadie meant to rule whatever husband she selected, absence of backbone and presence of "race" seemed just what was required.

It annoyed her to find out before they all reached the Plaza Hotel that he was already engaged to Nadine.

But this did not altogether prevent Sadie from endeavouring to attract him, and she said some lively things to entertain him during dinner.

The lights and the music had an effect upon Nadine: she blossomed forth and was gay and natural, and Mr. Bronson thought her a charming person.

A young man friend of Sadie's joined the party when they went to take their coffee in the hall, and at once Sadie suggested that they should go into the ball-room and dance.

Nadine's eyes began to flash with excitement; would her father let her do this unheard-of thing? He seemed to be making no objection, and off they started.

The room was half-empty, and Sadie thought it a miserable out-of-season show, but to Nadine it was a whirl of excitement.

She would dance for the first time with a *man!*

Eustace had already asked Sadie, and they were going ahead in a fox-trot, and the young man who had joined them placed his arm round Nadine.

Her feet felt as if they were shod in Mercury's sandals, her lithe body swayed to the syncopated rhythm, and her blue eyes flashed fiercely.

When the music stopped, she came up to Sir Edward looking like a radiant, brilliant flower; all her diffidence had departed, and for the first time she felt that she was attractive and was influencing men.

"It is just too divine to dance, Papa," she whispered. "I never want to go back to England and dull old home."

The young American was a perfect dancer, like most of his race, and the vast difference Nadine found in Eustace, when his turn came, brought her sharply back to earth again.

He had no idea of rhythm, and went round in measured time.

"Oh, it is no use," she said at last, exasperated, and stopped abruptly in the middle of the floor.

Her betrothed was surprised, but wanted to be kind.

"Of course, you cannot expect to know how to dance, Nadine, as this is only your first time. But do not be discouraged, my dear child; after a little practice you will get into it and learn to keep time."

Then she went into one of her fits of laughter, to Eustace's annoyed dismay.

"Why, it is you who have not a notion of what dancing means," she said, panting. "One might as well go round with an old broom."

Mr. Pelham drew himself up stiffly.

"I am sorry you find me like an old broom; let us go and sit down until the new one can again sweep you off your feet."

Oh, how like her father he looked when he said that! The same sarcastic, freezing tone; between the two of them, everything which gave her any pleasure in life was always spoilt.

And with a pettish shrug she took refuge at Sir Edward's side.

"Why are you not dancing, my dear?" he asked.

"Because Eustace thinks I cannot dance, and I think he cannot, so we have decide to sit down."

Fortunately, at that moment Sadie Bronson came up, and the two girls changed partners again.

And while Sir Edward watched his daughter his thoughts were troubled.

She and Eustace did not seem to agree over one single thing.

❃   ❃   ❃

Everything about America pleased Nadine.

She liked its newness, its noise, its rush, and its life.

When they got onto the private car in the train, her delight was to sit on the observation platform at the end and watch the country slipping away into perspective.

She had a charming little compartment all to herself to sleep in, and when everyone was taking a siesta after lunch, in the great heat as they began to get into the desert, she took out the *Story of Bayard*—the book went everywhere with her!

No, it was not this Bayard she wanted. Eustace, if he had a nicer character, could be this kind

36

of knight. To make her love him, a man must be much more affectionate, more dashing, more of a master.

Would she ever meet such a man? When it was too late? Then she fell asleep and dreamed of snakes!

Just before they were due at Albuquerque a day or so later, the usual game of bridge was going on.

Eustace was a tiresome player, taking a long time to make up his mind, and even Sadie grew impatient with him; while, if Nadine was his partner, she drummed her fingers on the table.

Fortunately, she felt that the confined conditions of a private car did not make *tête-à-tête* inevitable.

If one wanted that, one would have to arrange it with intelligence, as Sadie did to secure Eustace in the starlight after dinner.

Nadine was so absorbed with her own desire not to be with him that she had not observed Miss Bronson's machinations. But Blenkie had, and she was determined to defeat them.

Blenkie and her eternal knitting seemed never to be absent from the young people's horizon, but Sadie was more than a match for her, and often saw Eustace alone.

On this particular morning Mr. Bronson made the fourth at the game of bridge, while Sir Edward wrote letters and Blenkie knitted.

Suddenly Sadie looked up and cried excitedly:

"Oh, here we are in the Indian country. Come along and look at them when we get into the station at Albuquerque!"

Nadine rushed to her cabin for her camera,

and after they had drawn up she climbed down from the car using the other door.

Eustace and Sadie were far down the platform by now, buying trinkets of Indian silver. Blenkie was looking anxiously from the door, having lost sight of her charge.

Sir Edward and Mr. Bronson had not emerged from the drawing-room. Nadine, in delight at being alone, went up under one of the archways to photograph a squaw and a little papoose, who, for a dollar-piece for the baby's hand, were induced to pose.

Just as Nadine had fixed the sight to take the photograph, a tall young man came through the arch from the bookstall and paused for a moment, as if looking for some particular part of the train; he was exactly in focus, and the flash of recognition which came to Nadine coincided with the snap of the shutter.

This was the same face which had looked up at her from the side-door entrance at Pelham Court only six weeks before.

The young man was quite unconscious of having got in the way, until the squaw indignantly waved him aside, and then he realized what he had done.

With a murmured apology and a raise of his cap, he walked on.

Nadine gazed after him, forgetting to take another photograph. Where was he going?

The chattering of the squaw diverted her attention for one moment, and when she looked again she had lost sight of the man.

With a feeling of annoyance, she posed the Indian once more, and then walked briskly along the platform to join Eustace and Sadie.

Before she could reach them she caught sight of the young man again; he was carrying a small valise now. She watched intently, and saw that he was certainly going to get onto the train.

Oh, what a pity that he wasn't a gentleman and they would never meet . . . but what was this? He was actually entering their private car! A delicious feeling of excitement came over her. Who . . . who could he be?

What if Mumford had been mistaken and he was a gentleman after all?

With beating heart and pleasurable curiosity, she made her way to the drawing-room, where they all generally sat, and there through the doorway she could see the stranger in amicable conversation with her father and Mr. Bronson.

She crept quietly in and sat down on the low sofa in the background, but in a moment they grew conscious of her presence, and Sir Edward called to her.

"Come, Nadine, I want to introduce Mr. Delaval to you. My daughter—Mr. Delaval."

Nadine shyly shook hands with him and they sat down.

"Mr. Delaval knows all about gold and silver and other nice things, Miss Nadine," Mr. Bronson said. "When we get to Gold Stamp he is going to take us down the mine."

Some paper that Mr. Delaval had given them seemed of great interest to the two elderly gentlemen, and so while they studied it at the other end of the saloon, for a few moments Nadine was left in peace to talk to the young man.

His grey eyes were the first ones she had ever realized were looking at her with interest, and a second perfectly delicious thrill came over her.

"I hope you will be interested in this rough country that we are going to, Miss Pelham," he said.

She looked up at him.

"Indeed, yes, I know that I shall. Do you live there? I mean, is it your home?"

"No, my home is down in the South." He smiled quietly. "I am just up here because I am interested in mines."

"Tell me about them."

To Bayard Delaval, her blue eyes, set rather up at the corners, looked like stars at night, peering out of the thickest possible black lashes.

Her fine ivory-olive skin seemed as smooth as a tea-rose petal, with the faint scarlet flush growing in her cheeks.

Could lips be as red as that, he wondered, without a scrap of paint?

Yes, the whole thing was real!

She was so unutterably different from any of the other girls whom he knew—all the loveliest débutantes in Washington and New York, and all the rough, free-and-easy pals of the mining camps.

There was no calculation in this face, nothing "cute," just a beautiful, human, passionate creature who evidently felt an interest in him, as he did in her.

Women had not mattered very much to Bayard Delaval. They had been delightful to pass the rare times of his leisure with; they were merely the decorations of life, not the real objective.

To do, to achieve, was his aim. To wrest from nature a great fortune, which should give him power, and complete freedom, and presently a voice in his country's government.

He had not had the luck to get over to France during the war, but had been kept grinding at immense works for armament, where his special knowledge had been indispensable. That had been a bitter disappointment, for he had longed to fight.

Now, at thirty-three, life was opening for him in a vast way.

He had a one-fourth interest in the Gold Stamp Corporation, and was practically king out there at the mine.

A quiet, reserved, strong character, whom it was wiser not to quarrel with, and more advantageous to obey.

Responsibility and self-reliance create personality; there was nothing bashful or self-conscious about Bayard Delaval.

He took a comprehensive look at Nadine. Did she really want to hear about the mine, or was it just to make conversation?

"It is all so very rough, and different from anything that I expect you have been introduced to. We shall get to a part of the country presently where there is not a blade of grass, not a living tree or flower, just sage brush worse than the desert you have come through.

"And the air is scorching and thick with dust where men delve into the earth every day in search of gold."

"It sounds awful," whispered Nadine. "I do not care a bit about money."

"No, I suppose not."

A merry twinkle came into his keen eyes as he looked at her very perfect frock.

He knew that that kind of exquisite simplicity was the most expensive of all; he had often had to pay for it on his trips to New York, when he went back into the civilization of his old world again!

He looked at her perfect silk stockings and shoes and at the string of big pearls round her throat. Sir Edward thought pearls quite suitable for a girl, and had given her three on every birthday, which now made a perfect necklace.

"No, I suppose money has no significance for you," Bayard Delaval said again, and he laughed.

Nadine never liked people laughing at her. She pouted a little.

"I mean . . . of course, one has to have things."

"Yes, one has to have things, and the worst of it is that only such a few of those things that one wants are unaffected and uninfluenced by gold."

"I want freedom, and that has nothing to do with gold!"

"I want freedom too, but it, of all things, is concerned with gold."

"How?"

"Freedom implies liberty to do what you like, and to go where you like. Well, you can't stir more than a few miles without gold, and you can't make anyone help you without gold.

"If either of us were to be dropped off this train now, having been told we had perfect liberty, what would become of us without gold?

"We'd be dead of starvation and thirst in a day or so; but with gold we could bribe that

Indian you see over there to help us back into some civilization, where we could board a train again."

Nadine frowned.

"It is civilization which I believe I hate. I thing those Indians look delicious."

"I don't believe you would like their dirty huts, nor, being a woman, having to do all the hard work." He smiled.

"I see you are going to make me say that I don't really want freedom." And Nadine smiled now. "Well, tell me what your idea of freedom is."

"Freedom is when the spirit's desires are unhampered by material obstacles."

"Oh, that must be wonderful!" she said with a sigh.

"But the possession of sufficient gold is necessary to remove obstacles."

"For instance?"

"A man who has to work all day in a mine cannot be said to be free to indulge his spirit's desires; he probably longs to be out in the air, or enjoying some sport, or giving pleasure to the girl he loves, or . . ."

"Yes, I see."

"He goes on working and working to earn enough gold to make him free."

"How can a woman be free?"

"Women can never be free."

"You, an American, to say that! Why, Miss Sadie Bronson, who is with us on this trip, says that all American women are perfectly free and the men are slaves to them!"

He laughed again, showing very white teeth.

"The question is, have they got what their

43

spirits want, or have they only material freedom? And are there some obstacles which they cannot overcome either with gold or with cunning?

"For no matter what the obstacle may be, the knowledge that it is there precludes freedom."

Nadine thought of Sadie's words. How she longed for forbidden fruit!

No, even Sadie, rich, highly indulged Sadie, was as yet without the attainment of her heart's desire, she had not complete freedom!

"Then women cannot come so near to freedom as men?"

"No, they have to depend upon men for nearly everything that they really want."

He looked straight into Nadine's eyes, so she suddenly looked down, and her heart beat a little faster.

No one had ever talked to her like this before. The guests, who came to Pelham Court, who were of her own station in life, treated her always as a child.

Eustace, as someone of so little interest that conversation with her was too fatiguing to continue for long.

She had never met any young men, other than the parson's son, and one or two youths of the neighbourhood who were sometimes asked to play tennis but never left to talk to her!

She found herself interested as she had never been before in her life.

She had a sudden feeling that she would like him to show mastery, and she had no sense of rebellion, which was always uppermost when she was with her father.

Bayard Delaval had been analyzing her. Here

was a nature as yet unawakened, but what a well of passion lay deep there in her eyes!

He found himself greatly moved. How dull and grey and commonplace his life had been of late!

He bent a little nearer to her.

"This evening after dinner I want to show you what the desert means in the starlight. Will you come out on the observation platform?"

But before Nadine could answer, Miss Blenkensop came upon them from her compartment, her knitting in her hands!

Blenkie at once sensed a danger. If Sir Edward wanted his daughter to marry her cousin Eustace, it was obviously her duty, as duenna, not to allow any attractive interlopers to intervene!

So she sat down in the most upright chair that she could see.

Mr. Delaval took her measure.

"It would be pretty hard to put anything over on her!" he decided, silently.

Nadine felt excited but she did not know why.

How would they be able to arrange their afternoon?

She would pretend that she was going to have the usual siesta, and indeed she would lie down for a few moments, to allay Blenkie's watchfulness, and then she would get up and creep quietly through the two saloons to the observation platform; and even if Mr. Delaval was engaged with her father and Mr. Bronson, he would see her as she passed and possibly make some excuse to get away from them and join her.

Blenkie saw her safely to her berth and felt reassured. She had heard Sir Edward say at lunch-

45

eon that they would examine reports afterwards.

Sadie had apparently gone to her compartment. It seemed that the watchdog would be allowed to rest!

Nadine got Augustine to come as soon as she knew that Blenkie was safely off, and she changed her frock to a more becoming one; then she took a book and walked through the saloon.

She was a little piqued because not one of the three men seemed to notice her passage. She did not stop to exchange words with Sadie and Eustace, who appeared to be innocently playing dominoes in the drawing-room.

It was awfully hot out there on the observation platform and she was glad that she had brought an umbrella.

She settled herself and tried to read, and once or twice she nearly fell off to sleep. It was getting late, tea would come, and Blenkie, and there would probably not be another chance!

A feeling of disappointment arose in her, and then resentment. Why were things so contrary?

Then just as she thought she must go and see what was happening, the door opened and Mr. Delaval came out. He stretched himself in the basket chair beside her.

"I knew that you were still here, of course," he said. "I have never before found it hard to keep my attention on my work."

"And you find it difficult now? It certainly is hot."

"I wanted to be out here, in the air."

His eyes were smiling at her. Then they both laughed.

"I came to your home about six weeks ago. I did not know about you then, or I believe I'd have lost the steamer and accepted your father's invitation to stay over the weekend!"

"Papa asked you and you did not stay? Oh, if you only had ..."

She suddenly blushed as she realized that she had said something indiscreet.

"Would it have made any difference, then, if I had stayed?"

He was certainly surprised.

"It might have.... Eu ... we had a party arriving that afternoon, and some of them were such dull people. It might all have been more fun if you had stayed."

He knew that this was not the real reason, and that if he were to probe what it really was it would embarrass her.

He was very tempted to do so, but, he let it pass for the moment.

"You have a gorgeous home, Miss Pelham," he said instead.

"I saw you out the window. The windows of my room look over the side door."

Mr. Delaval leaned over nearer to her.

"I remember I did look up, and I thought I saw someone looking from behind a curtain for a second, as though they were expecting someone."

Nadine clasped her hands suddenly, and then she felt her engagement ring.

She was glad that it was hidden! How she hated to think that she was bound to Eustace!

Bayard Delaval was wondering. There was evidently some memory connected with this visit of his to Pelham Court, but what could it be?

Nadine did not want him to ask her, so she began to talk quickly.

"What did you think of Pelham?"

"It must be a wonderful thing to own a place like that, to remember when you are walking round that the trees have been yours since they sprung from the earth, and that every bit of it is full of memories. Your father must be a very proud man."

"He is. But oh, Mr. Delaval, you can't think what it is to live under all these memories. They crush you. I never feel that I belong to them. I am quite different: my mother was a Russian, you know."

"Ah! I was wondering what it was. You don't look English. What a strange force heredity is. Then the things your father values don't mean much to you, do they?"

"Not a great deal." And she looked out at the vanishing track. "I want to live, and not be suffocated by tradition. I want to form and expand my own opinions."

Bayard Delaval leaned forward again and looked at her. What a very pleasant task it would be to assist such a girl to emancipation!

"Do they keep you tied up?"

"Oh, I ought not to grumble. Papa is very kind, and so is everyone else. But it is the same thing every day and always.

"One must do certain things because the Pelhams have always done them. Or, one must not do certain things because the Pelhams have never done them.

"The Pelham name, the Pelham name! Sometimes I'd rather be called Smith!"

"I don't know—to have a name means a

standard to live up to. Over here we value those things quite a good deal. But they don't amount to a red cent unless character goes with them."

Nadine looked at him and a thrill ran through her. He was so strong and lithe, and his mouth was so firm.

She *felt* that he knew how to command and was afraid of nothing on earth. Ah, if only they had lived in the olden days, he would indeed have been a knight. . . .

"Tea is ready," said Eustace, putting his head through the door. "Aren't you people going to have any?"

"The English cannot live without their tea," Nadine said, "so of course I must go in."

Very reluctantly she rose.

"This track seems to me like life," she said, as she leaned over the rail and watched the objects at each side gradually diminishing until they melted into the blue distance.

"Things seem frightfully large and in no time they have just got so small they don't matter a bit."

"Everything depends upon the point of view, and sometimes when things are close to us our passions magnify them out of all porportion, and it is only when we see them in perspective that we can realize how foolish we have been."

"Miss Blenkensop says that no one ought to indulge in passion, it distorts everything."

"There are passions—and passions," he said, and there was a look in his eyes which made Nadine say quickly:

"Let's go to tea."

Chapter
Three

Miss Blenkensop wondered why Nadine never took off her gloves at tea. She ate nothing, to be sure, so it was not necessary, and besides, Blenkie herself had always encouraged the wearing of gloves.

"If he did see the ring at luncheon, then it can't be helped," Nadine was thinking. "But if he did not, then he shan't until the last possible moment."

So she went without some wonderful hot cakes the cook had made, and kept her loosely gloved little hands in her lap.

Nadine was very small for an English girl, not over five feet two inches, and her feet and hands were the tiniest possible.

Mr. Delaval had not admired the statuesque Englishwomen during his visit. His attitude towards women was protective, and he perferred the size that he could pick up in his arms.

Miss Bronson was most sprightly at tea. Her sophisticated comprehension had taken in that Nadine was interested in the young engineer, and she did not intend that there should be any pauses in the conversation or any chance that this interest should show.

It would suit her plans very well if, presently, Nadine's conduct could be used as a lever to separate her from Eustace. But at the present moment, to arouse his jealousy, or rather his wounded vanity, might reawaken his interest in his fiancée.

So, for her own ends, Sadie played into the hands of fate, and aided the pair to circumvent Blenkie again.

The four went out onto the observation platform, and then they divided two and two at the far sides, the noise of the train quite preventing either couple from overhearing the other's conversation.

"Do you like dancing, Miss Pelham?" Mr. Delaval asked. "We do such a lot of it here."

"I adore it, but I have hardly ever danced with anyone. I am not what is called 'out' in England ... that is, I have not been presented at Court, or been to a real ball yet. I danced with a young man for the first time in New York.

"Eustace, my cousin, does not think I know how. He is precise, like all the rest of the family, and steps in measured time, dum-dum-dum.

"It says absolutely nothing to me; I want to forget all about everything but the rhythm."

She half-shut her eyes, voluptuously, and her nostrils quivered. She was entirely unconscious that she was presenting a sensuously attractive picture to any young man sitting next to her. She was not thinking of herself or of what effect she was producing.

Something in her nature was awakening, that was all.

Bayard Delaval thrilled. He knew now that he

was falling in love with her. And what would this
lead to?

Sir Edward Pelham would never consider
him as a son-in-law, even though he was quite rich
enough now to make a very presentable settle-
ment and he would be very much richer indeed in
the near future.

But one of another nation!

No, he knew that the very idea would appear
to Sir Edward as impossible.

This, however, was no great obstacle. A girl
had a right to please herself, and if he should be
able to make her love him, no father could stand
in the way.

Like Blenkie's opposition, her father's an-
tagonism would make Nadine more precious.

All this flashed through his head in the few
seconds while he was looking at her red, full
mouth, as she spoke of dancing.

He intended to enjoy every moment, whether
anything further came of it or not.

They talked of travel after this; neither had
seen the continent of Europe, and they both longed
to explore Italy and Spain.

"I can't think of anything more divine," Nadine said, "than to go to Italy, with plenty of time,
and a nice motor."

Then, as she saw the look of awakening emotion in his face, she went on hurriedly:

"And . . . and . . . a nice party of people who
like it too."

"I don't think I should want a party. I would
like to go just with one person whom I love."

His voice, which was very deep, had many
insinuating tones in it.

Nadine's imagination took fire at once. That was the sort of trip she too would wish for.

"Tell me where you would go first!" she said a little breathlessly. "In . . . Italy, I mean."

"Well, supposing we made Genoa our head-quarters, landing there from here. Then I suppose one would go north to Milan, and Florence.

"Florence must be wonderful, a city of merchant princes, like us Americans. I would like to study the Italian Renaissance on the spot, wouldn't you?"

"Oh, yes," whispered Nadine, whose thoughts had centred not so much on the pleasure of studying history but on the intoxicating joy of having a charming lover in ideal surroundings!

Her eyes were shining.

"I suppose there are some people in the world who can realize their dreams and go on trips like that."

" 'Never the time, and the place, and the loved one, all together,' " he quoted lightly. "But I don't believe in the word 'never.'

"I believe if you want a thing, and it is the right thing for you, that just to determine to go out and get it, and not let the grass grow under your feet, always gets you there in the end.

"Perhaps someday, Miss Pelham, both you and I will realize our dreams."

He was looking at her so intently now that she dared not look up. She had a feeling that something was tempting her to move very close to him.

"Well, and after Florence, where then?" she asked, after a little while, with a pout.

She had been wondering why he was silent.

54

He was not becoming like Eustace, she hoped,
uninterested in everything she said.

"Well, we'd go to Pisa and see the Leaning
Tower."

Something quivered in her when he said
"we'd"; did he mean he and she?

"And we would get down to Rome, and the
South, and I guess we'd be feeling pretty pagan by
then, and have a look at Greece."

"I can't imagine anything more delightful,"
exclaimed Nadine. "If ... if ... the party was sym-
pathetic, and wanted the same things.

"My governess and Papa and I always want
something different. It would not be any fun to go
with them."

"Let's pretend we are going together, just you
and me."

The scarlet-pink flush came into her cheeks,
and she felt that she must chaff now, for she was
feeling so deeply.

"I'm horrid to travel with ... so capricious.
You would not like it a bit."

"I should not let you be capricious. A woman
is not capricious if she is handled the right way."

"You know a great deal about women, Mr.
Delaval?"

"A pretty considerable amount. They are
predatory animals, as a rule, cunning as foxes,
brave as lions, slippery as eels."

"What do they want?"

"A master, and ..."

"Pouff!" Nadine interrupted, tossing her head
in mock indignation.

"You did not let me finish, I'd got as far as
'and.' "

"Well, and what?"

"Lots of love."

Nadine looked down suddenly and clasped her hands; she felt her engagement ring. Yes, this was true, lots of love.

This American man had put her unconscious longings into words. That is what she wanted of life, this great wonderful thing which mattered far more than anything else in the world.

When she looked up again her blue eyes were a little fierce.

"Some people do not seem to be allowed any of that, they are just made to do their duty all the time. I have often wondered, what is love?"

"It is the best thing in life. Half the folks who talk about it don't really know what it means, they fritter it all away on silly little sensations.

"We ought never to be satisfied until we have found someone who makes up the whole show for us, and then we should give the best and the greatest of our being.

"But love for me means fidelity. I'm like your Marquis of Montrose in the song:

"A woman would have to be utterly mine in word and thought and look. I'd never stand any other fellow hanging round.

"If I gave her the whole of my heart, I'd want the whole of hers."

Nadine felt that a great breath of desert air was rushing round her and almost sweeping her off her feet.

Passion blazed in her eyes as she turned towards the young man, but she caught sight of Eustace beyond him, reclining, with his usual indifferent lassitude; Sadie was doing all the talking.

This was her fate, a boneless, flabby, over-civilized partner for life, whom in the end she should rule and break into bits . . . and beside her was a master. . . .

Bayard Delaval knew that they were on very dangerous ground and that he must not let them go too far at present. He had an instant longing to take her in his arms and teach her all about love.

But his will was a strong one. So he held back the burning words.

The sun was beginning to sink in the west, the line had taken a curve for the last mile, and they seemed to be facing the great orange ball of fire.

Nadine looked over the sage brush to the endless desert, and sighed.

"I wonder why the evening is so much more beautiful than the day, and yet always a little sad. The desert is hideous at noontime, and now it looks all mysterious and enticing."

"Illusion. The desert is the same, only the low sun makes the shadows and the colours beautiful, and that is why it is sad. We know it is only illusion, really."

Nadine rose.

"Let us come away out of illusion, back into the reality of dressing for dinner."

He got up with her, and held the door open for her to pass into the drawing-room beyond, and as he did so a lurch of the car threw her a little against him, so that he caught the scent of her hair.

"It is a good thing it isn't dark!" he thought, as he turned and sat down again.

When Nadine reached her compartment she

sank into a chair. She felt that she must not let herself think. She *would* not think.

She was going to put on an especially becoming frock, and she was going to enjoy her evening, come what might!

* * *

As Nadine went down the passage to the saloon for dinner, she kept twisting her engagement ring. Then she left it with the stone inside; the little platinum circle might not catch the eye as much as the big diamond, was her half-conscious thought.

She placed herself opposite Mr. Delaval, a little obliquely, when they sat down to the table, so that the flowers might hide her hands.

She was demure all through the meal, rather silent, only talking occasionally to Mr. Bronson, on her right.

Bayard Delaval was no young college lad accustomed to giving way to all his feelings. He showed no special interest in Miss Pelham now.

Indeed, he had some lively sallies with Sadie Bronson, who was always full of back talk. So, the dinner passed without any of the powers having had their suspicions aroused.

Would Mr. Delaval really be able to manoeuvre that they two could again go and sit on the observation platform? This was all Nadine was thinking about.

Mr. Delaval apparently had some important plans of the mine to look up in his cabin, and asked to be excused the moment dinner was over.

The two elderly gentlemen and Sadie and

Eustace settled down to bridge and Blenkie to her knitting.

Nadine's heart sank. He might at least have *tried* to see her and talk to her! She went into her cabin and fetched the *Story of Bayard,* and she sat down in the rear saloon, whose door opened onto the platform.

She had not been there very long, however, when Mr. Delaval came back with some papers; but, seeing the bridge party made up, he could not, of course, disturb them.

So in the most casual way he strolled past Blenkie and on to the farther saloon, and there, as though merely for the sake of politeness, he took a chair next to Nadine.

His keen grey eyes were whimsical.

"If you are in the middle of a wood, and want to get to a place at the right end of it, you've sometimes got to go out at the left and come round. Do you know that, Miss Pelham?"

Nadine laughed.

"Especially when there are dragons and foxes and sheep in the wood."

He glanced at Blenkie's uncompromising back, which could be seen through the doors.

"She never leaves you, I suppose?"

"Never. Can't you understand why I am always talking about freedom?"

"Yes . . . What is that book you are reading?"

"It is the one that I love best in the world. It is the *Story of Bayard* . . . my knight."

He leaned forward eagerly. Could she have said that on purpose? But no, she probably did not know his name—he would tell her.

"My name is Bayard," he said.

Nadine was thoroughly startled. That mystic side of her nature, inherited from her gipsy mother, concerned itself a great deal with omens and co-incidences.

"Your name...is...Bayard? How extraordinary!"

She gasped a little between the words, while the colour came into her cheeks.

"If you only knew how awfully strange that is!"

Nadine was staring at him while she unconsciously clasped the book to her breast, forgetting about showing the ring.

Surely there was fate in this!

She had called him Bayard, her knight, come to set her free, when she had seen him out the window...and his real name was Bayard! Did coming events cast their shadows beforehand?

The confusion which she was in showed on her face.

Mr. Delaval was really intrigued. There was something about his going to Pelham that day, and his name, which evidently had power to cause this lovely girl great emotion. He would try to find out what it could be.

"Please, will you tell me why it is so odd that my name should be Bayard?" he asked, bending over nearer to her.

His action caught the attention of Blenkie, who was keeping her eye upon them from the other saloon.

An interesting conversation with anyone but her fiancé should not be encouraged in her pupil, this good governess felt; she began picking up a stitch in her knitting, preparatory to joining them.

Bayard Delaval realized that there was no time to be lost.

"Won't you tell me?" he pleaded.

Then, before Nadine could answer, he saw the ring on her left third finger, and his face hardened, and a question grew in his eyes, which were fixed on her hand clasping the book.

She realized what had happened, with a strange pang at her heart, and quickly dropped the book with both hands in her lap, while she lowered her head so that he could not see her eyes.

"You are engaged to someone, Miss Pelham?"

His voice sounded a little hoarse even to himself.

"To ... my cousin ... Eustace," Nadine whispered almost inaudibly.

He began to speak, but Miss Blenkensop was upon them with some appropriate remark about the weather.

So Bayard Delaval crushed back all the wild things which he might have said, and got up, vacating his place, which Blenkie immediately filled.

"I think there is going to be a thunderstorm," he said, and glanced out the window. Then he strolled back to the others at the bridge-table.

For once Nadine gave way to her feelings. She could have killed Blenkie!

"Can't you ever leave me alone?" she cried angrily, and, bounding up with her precious book, she went out into the night, slamming the platform door after her.

Miss Blenkensop was too dumbfounded and horrified to express herself, and dropped two stitches in her knitting!

When the cool air blew upon Nadine's face, she put up her hand and loosened her hair in the front, letting the wind blow through it. It seemed as though it could help her to think.

All pleasure was over; he now knew that she was tied and bound to Eustace, and he would show no more interest in her. How hateful everything was!

The overmastering influence of her father still held her so strongly that she never once thought of open rebellion. She could storm and rage, but the idea of breaking chains never occurred to her.

And by the bridge-table Bayard Delaval was cursing fate. Why had he not noticed the ring before?

He did not suppose that she had deliberately hidden it from him, as indeed why should she?

They had only met that morning for the first time, so he could not yet matter to her enough for her to have wished to deceive him. No, it was just his own stupidity.

Engaged to Eustace Pelham! A family arrangement, of course. In Europe they still did things like that, he supposed.

Of course the girl could not care for such a fellow; and he looked down at Eustace's delicate hands holding the cards.

But at least until he knew that the engagement was against her wish, it would not be the straight thing to do to make up to her.

He would stick to friendship, and grow to know her mind.

But since she was brimming with passion, and life, and was quite unaware of it, or that there was danger ahead, it would be wiser not to court temptation by going out onto the observation platform to look at the stars, as had been his intention.

Sadie Bronson, however, disposed of matters in her own way. She was "out" for the moment and leaned back in her chair.

"Oh, isn't it hot, Mr. Delaval?" she said. "Let's go and get a breath of air."

Then she rose and went to the platform door, and the young man was obliged to follow her.

They found Nadine leaning over the rail, gazing at the stars, a heavy black cloud seeming to make those below it more bright.

"I wonder what they mean?" she said, pointing to the sky. "Are they really worlds, or only angels' eyes watching us?"

"How tired they must get night after night for thousands of years, seeing the same old games. But I never did think angels had much of a time anyway," Miss Bronson remarked.

"It is the devils who get all the candies."

Then, after a few more pertinent sentences, she turned back to the door again.

"You'd better give Miss Pelham a lesson in astronomy, Mr. Delaval. . . . 'Up above the world so high, like a diamond in the sky.' . . . I'm for spades and clubs in the saloon!"

"And how about hearts, Miss Bronson? What will you do with them?" he asked, as he held the door for her.

"I'll leave them for you to play with on the observation platform, Mr. Delaval!" And with a saucy backwards glance she went from them.

Nadine was very nervous. She felt that she must talk at once so as to avoid anything serious.

63

She was so inexperienced, she had no idea of leading a conversation in the way she would have wished, so she blurted out:

"Isn't Sadie a delightful person, so full of fun. I wish I were an American girl. . . ."

"I don't! You are much more interesting as you are, there is so much to discover in you."

"I don't think that I know myself."

"I am sure you do not. You may give yourself a great surprise someday."

"I suppose it is wrong of me to have such instincts, but I so often get wild feelings that I must just run away and live like a gipsy.

"And, do you know, there are some kinds of music which drive me crazy!"

"You are half Russian, didn't you say?"

He was thinking she looked like a gipsy there under the stars, with the yellow light falling upon her dimly from the saloon windows behind.

Her olive-ivory skin, and very black hair, ruffled and curly now, where she had loosened it, appeared so extremely un-English.

"Yes, my mother was a Russian princess. I suppose Papa loved her very much, because he never speaks of her. She died when I was only a year old."

(No one had ever told Nadine that her mother was a gipsy.)

"I put flowers on her tomb every Saturday when we are at home."

She sighed, and then the door opened and Sir Edward came out.

He had looked up from his bridge when Miss Bronson returned, and suddenly became aware of both his daughter's and the young mining engineer's absence from the saloon beyond, while Miss Blenkensop could be seen knitting agitatedly by the outer door.

The rubber had ended a moment or two after, and he rose while they were shuffling the cards, and came to her.

"Where is Nadine, Miss Blenkensop?" he asked, a little sternly.

"She has remained upon the balcony with Mr. Delaval, Sir Edward. In spite of incurring her anger, I was just about to join them."

Sir Edward frowned.

"Why should she be angry at your coming?"

"I regret to say Nadine quite lost her temper just now, and reproached me for never leaving her alone."

Blenkie's knitting needles flashed fiercely, she moved them so rapidly.

Sir Edward lit a cigarette, then he opened the balcony door.

What he saw was two young backs leaning over the rail, and Mr. Delaval was pointing to the north as though explaining something.

This seemed innocent enough, but Sir Edward knew the world and the nature of man, even if that of woman was a fearsome mystery to him.

He had come out just in time, he decided. Bayard Delaval turned to him without the least embarrassment.

"By tomorrow evening we shall be at Gold Stamp," he announced. "It is there to the north-east."

"Isn't it all delightful?" Nadine said.

She was far from feeling calm. She feared her father would be displeased with her, and that frightened her, and she was chilled by the stiffness which had come into Mr. Delaval's tones.

Yes, all fun was over. He would not bother with her now that he knew she was engaged.

And because he had become not only forbidden fruit, which he had been from the beginning, but out of her reach as well, her interest in him had begun to grow proportionately.

Every woman probably has felt at some time in her life just what Nadine was experiencing.

All the wild part of her nature was seething, and all the part that was fear of her father held it in check.

"It is quite time that you were in bed, child," Sir Edward said. "It is after ten, and you have had a long day."

When she had gone, he talked at length to his chief engineer, and, being a just man, if filled with old-fashioned prejudices, he was obliged to admit to himself that he was a very intelligent fellow.

In spite of his American slang, which was so apt as to be interesting, he was quite unaccountably a gentleman!

"Delaval?" Sir Edward said to himself. "From decent stock, undoubtedly. I wonder if he knows from which branch he has come."

Nadine had literally bounced past Miss Blenkensop and had given Eustice a frigid good-night.

Augustine was waiting for her mistress but was quickly dismissed; and then when she was alone Nadine threw herself down upon the sofa, and angry tears scorched her eyes.

His name was Bayard. Surely fate in some way *must* be going to make him her knight!

66

But he did not seem at all interested now. He had talked of such a lot of technical things.

Not of the stars, nor had he insisted that she should tell him why it was odd that his name should be what it was.

She felt that she hated Eustace. She hated Blenkie. She almost hated her father. But here her thoughts stopped in fear again.

There would never be any getting away from Papa.

Her senses seemed to be all on the alert.

It almost seemed that, in spite of the noise of the train, she could hear the gramophone ... Victrola, Sadie called it ... and was she dreaming, or was it playing that Russian music which she had heard on the ship?

She jumped up and opened her door a little. Yes, now she could hear more plainly.

She undid the few pins in her rather short, curly hair, and shook it out.

Then she began to dance. The music was very indistinct, and presently she sank again into a low chair.

❀　　❀　　❀

Sir Edward and Miss Blenkensop prevented a moment's *tête-à-tête* between Mr. Delaval and Nadine until they arrived at bustling, busy Gold Stamp.

And because it was a human agency and not fate which had intervened, some stubborn quality in the young man came uppermost, and made him determine to make opportunities for himself!

He could not bear the idea of Sir Edward and that stern governess getting the better of him!

The Gold Stamp Hotel was like all American hotels of mushroom growth, filled with every convenience, if devoid of beauty.

But there was a ball-room with a good floor and a stirring band, which played rhythmic, syncopated music.

Nadine noticed that everywhere Bayard Delaval went, he was greeted with cordial respect.

She made herself look as lovely as possible in the simplest of her Paris frocks, for dinner, and came down with Miss Blenkensop hoping that something would turn up.

She had fretted like a horse on too tight a curb all the day in the train, knowing full well that her father now had instructed Blenkie to circumvent any possible talks with the young American.

But surely if Sadie suggested dancing after dinner they could not prevent her from dancing with him!

Sadie did suggest dancing, and although Sir Edward in his heart disapproved of *his* daughter dancing in the ball-room of a mining-town hotel, he was too courteous to cast a reflection upon his partner's child by forbidding his own from participating in the amusement.

"My dear boy, I think you had better look after Nadine," was merely all he said to Eustace.

Mr. Delaval, with great tact, had already asked Miss Bronson to dance, and the four started.

Nadine had difficulty controlling her temper. All joy had left her, her feet felt like lead, and Eustace said:

"You are dancing beautifully, Nadine. You see,

dear child, it was only because you were not used to my step; your time is perfect now."

"I am sure it is," she snapped rather bitterly.

That is just how life would be with him. Of course, they would all think her perfect when she had not a scrap of spirit left!

She watched Sadie and Mr. Delaval with the corner of her eye. It was plain to be seen that *he* knew all about dancing!

Oh, what would it be to whirl round in his arms like that. Would this tiresome old fox-trot never end. . . .

It did finish at the usual time, and the two couples joined each other.

Nadine had purposely stopped at the farther side of the room from where her father and Blenkie stood.

"Oh, Nadine, Mr. Delaval is too glorious to dance with . . . you just try!" Miss Bronson exclaimed ecstatically.

The pauses between the dances were extremely short, and as she spoke a valse struck up.

"I hate valses," Eustace announced. "Let us go and sit down, Miss Bronson."

Sadie complied, and Nadine found herself floating away in Mr. Delaval's arms!

If she had been exalted by the mere fact of dancing with the uninteresting young man in New York, she now felt almost intoxicated, her pleasure was so great.

Fate seemed to be benign to them for that evening! Mr. Bronson was engaging Sir Edward in deep conversation with a number of the mining magnates, and his back was turned to them.

Miss Blenkensop also had been introduced to a sheriff's wife.

The perfect rhythm of the valse carried the pair on in a kind of exquisite dream. Their hearts were beating close together.

They never paused for a second until the music stopped, and then both were a little pale.

Bayard Delaval was accustomed to controlling all his emotions, and his speech, so he said nothing ecstatic and held himself sternly in hand, but all these wonderful sensations were quite new to Nadine, and she could not successfuly hide them.

Her eyes were misty and soft with passion, and her lips looked like ripe cherries.

He knew very well that if they had been alone at that moment, nothing could have kept them from falling into each other's arms. . . .

He must not dance with her again that night. He *must* act up to his standard of a square game.

He knew quite well what she was feeling, and the temptation to tell her that he loved her was immense.

He tried to say something very ordinary, and asked if he might bring up one or two great friends of his who were in the hotel.

Nadine came down to earth. She curtseyed, and he took her across to Miss Blenkensop while he pretended to look for the young men.

He went outside into the night air, his temples feeling as though they were about to burst.

As he stood there, one of the very boys, Hickory Cannon, whom he intended to introduce, came up to him, and together they went back into the ball-room.

The introduction was made, and as Nadine

70

went off to dance with the newcomer, Bayard joined the group of elderly gentlemen.

Nadine felt deeply upset. He did not want to dance with her, then?

Had she not danced well, or was it only because he knew she was engaged? Her utterly untrained emotions were causing her anguish, almost.

She knew nothing about love or how it came to people. She had only her own imagination to guide her as to what it might be.

She had no conscious thought that she was in love with Bayard Delaval, she only knew, dumbly, like an animal, that every fibre of her being desired to be near him, and that she hated him to have gone off to her father, away from her, like that.

Perhaps she had shown Mr. Delaval too plainly that she had found the valse divine!

But what was the boy she was now dancing with saying about Bayard and a wonderful story of shooting and coolness of head?

"Do you mean that you really shoot people here?" Nadine asked, aghast.

"We did a little of that during the strikes last year."

"Oh, do tell me about it!" implored Nadine.

And so they stopped dancing and went and sat down, and Hickory Cannon began.

"Mr. Delaval . . . killed a man?"

Nadine's voice was awed, when he had finished.

"Why, certainly. That's why we respect him. He always stands for fair play, and isn't afraid to shoot to enforce it!"

Nadine thrilled . . . here was a master indeed!

71

She suddenly thought of Eustace, and then she laughed.

He came up just then, his conscience rather guilty because his acquaintance with Miss Bronson had, he began to be afraid, developed into a kind of flirtation!

Sadie had been extremely alluring during the valse they had sat out.

Meanwhile, Bayard Delaval was going through unwonted disturbance of mind. He had not felt this violent emotion towards a woman since he was a college lad.

He was angry with himself that anything should have such power over him. He hated to know that Nadine was now dancing with her fiancé.

He hated to think that anyone had the right to touch her!

He turned to the group of old gentlemen, and it chanced that Mr. Bronson drew him closer to the dancers, so that when Eustace and Nadine stopped, it was beside them.

And when the music began again Mr. Bronson was talking to Eustace, who seemed absorbed in what he was saying. Nadine could not keep a look of invitation from her eyes.

Bayard bent nearer to her, meaning to tell her that he had business to talk over with her father and must go, but she took it to mean that he would dance, so she placed her hand on his arm.

He knew that she was too timid and sensitive for him to say baldly that this had not been his intention, so there was nothing for it but to go on.

The moment he held her close to him, the same wild joy filled Nadine, and she turned her radiant face up to him in answer to some quite casual thing he had said, just as her father happened to join Mr. Bronson close to where they had paused.

It was a revelation to Sir Edward.

It was Nada looking at him all over again, as she stretched herself towards him along the table among the broken glass, with just the same voluptuous, passionate abandon.

Good God! What was to be done!

He could not say that the young man was presuming. There was no look of "come hither" in his face. Indeed, his closely cut features appeared rather stern.

He could not stop his daughter in the middle of the dance, but she should go to bed the moment it was finished!

And the next time they came round Nadine caught her father's icy glance, and the old fear returned to her, so she quickly made up her mind.

She would not wait for him to make some freezingly polite remark about the lateness of the hour, or some other excuse, but of her own accord she would go up to him and say she was tired.

Bayard Delaval felt the change in her, and he looked down and saw her full underlip quiver.

"What is the matter?" he asked, perhaps a little too tenderly. "The life seems suddenly to have gone out of your feet!"

"It has," she whispered. "I am tired. I think I will say good-night now."

They stopped close to her father and Nadine put out her hand.

"Good-night, Mr. Delaval," she said politely. "Papa, where is Blenkie? I suppose we shall have

73

to be up very early tomorrow to go to the mine, so we had better go to bed now."

Sir Edward was nonplussed—he did not expect this sensible decision on her part! He unfroze, and stood talking to her and the young mining engineer until Eustace and Blenkie came up and joined them.

"Aren't you tired, Blenkie?" Nadine said. "I am. Let's go."

And then they said good-night all round. Sir Edward found himself very much disturbed as he talked to Bayard Delaval and Mr. Bronson later on.

The young man was so sensible, so quiet, so resourceful. There was nothing in him to find fault with.

The only thing he, Sir Edward, could possibly do was to keep a more careful watch upon his daughter.

A sense almost of resentment came over him when he thought of Eustace. He was certainly not an ardent lover. He would give him a hint, at the first opportunity, to quicken his pace a bit.

They were to start at eight in the morning, in automobiles built especially to go over the rough, uneven ground, to go about fifty miles off to the new camp of Gold Rock, where the Gold Stamp Mining Corporation owned the wonderful new mine.

There they would stay for the night in an extremely primitive hotel.

At Gold Rock there would be horses, so those who wished could ride.

Mr. Delaval had arranged it all in the best way the limited resources of the place permitted.

But there were no side-saddles to be got in the whole town!

However, Miss Bronson had solved the difficulty. She had two American riding-suits with her, and one she would lend to Nadine to ride astride.

When the two girls had talked about it just before dinner, Nadine had been full of glee.

"Just fancy Papa's and Blenkie's faces when they see me in boots and breeches, Sadie! They will nearly die!"

"We must not let them catch a glimpse of us until we are starting! It will be enchanting fun."

Nadine's sleep that night was peaceful and sound, and she woke the next morning fresh and beautiful, with no foreboding or any presentiment that Fate in twenty-four hours would change her whole life.

Chapter Four

The morning was glorious and everybody seemed to be in the best of tempers at breakfast.

Eustace, who had been given a hint by Sir Edward, was a little more ardent in his attentions to Nadine.

He deliberately sat beside her in the automobile, with Blenkie beyond, leaving the Bronsons and Sir Edward and Mr. Delaval to go in another car when they started for the mine.

Nadine was going through what every girl has felt when she is first in love. She was conscious that she was very disappointed and that all her desires were for the young American.

The going was rough, the road a mere wagon-track, with deep ruts.

Gradually the cars began to get nearer the mountain and then commenced to climb.

Then at the summit a wonderful view met their eyes far down below again, a vast sea of sand with high mountains all round it, some snow-tipped, weirdly desolate.

Eustace made appropriate remarks now and

77

then, but Nadine was absolutely silent. Her whole mind now was set upon Bayard Delaval.

They passed several mule teams dragging water and provisions. The place they were going to produced neither.

When they came to a small gasoline filling station, the other car was waiting for them.

Whether or not the concentrated thoughts of the two young women, desiring a change of occupants, had anything to do with it, when they set out again Nadine was in the middle between her father and Mr. Delaval in one car, and Blenkie, Sadie, and Eustace were in the other, with Mr. Bronson beside the driver.

Sadie had probably arranged this with her usual tact. And now, the more bumpy the road, the more Nadine enjoyed herself.

Absolute thrills were running through her, as every girl experiences when physically close to the man she loves.

Mr. Delaval was being an intelligent guide. He talked principally to Sir Edward, but when some particularly wicked piece of road threw Nadine almost into his arms, she felt somehow that he was not unresponsive.

In her whole life she had never before been so happy as during that hour as they drove towards the rough mining camp.

It came in view at last, at about eleven o'clock, after they had come down from the mountain and crossed back to the sand plain of the desert.

Gold Rock was just a cluster of rough shanties, canvas lean-tos, tents, a few boarded stores, a sheriff's office, and a board hotel, which had been run up in the last four months.

Everybody was very interested and amused. And the ladies were shown to their rooms by the quaint western landlady, a desert character beloved by all the miners within miles.

What Mrs. O'Hara did not know about the natures of men was not worth mentioning!

"Come along, dearie," she said to the aghast Blenkie. " 'Tain't a palace, but we'll give ya the best we can."

Miss Blenkensop resented greatly being called "dearie" by such a "person."

But Nadine and Sadie delighted in the jolly, corpulent creature, and laughed heartily with her, when they had left Blenkie safely in her room.

The bedrooms were extremely primitive, but each had a private room, which was a rare luxury in these parts!

"Now what I've done," confided Sadie in Nadine's ear, "is to make Poppa get off in the motor with your father, leaving Mr. Pelham and Mr. Delaval to ride with us.

"They'll start first, because Mr. Delaval says the automobile road is much farther round than the track we shall take, so they won't see your get-up until we get to the mine.

"Sir Edward will be startled, won't he?"

Nadine was wild with excitement, and Sadie left her to change into the riding things.

Miss Blenkensop was to remain behind, as she had no head for swinging into the bowels of the earth, she confessed, and before the two girls emerged from their rooms onto the narrow landing, she had already retired for a much-needed rest.

Nadine felt very shy and very excited as she

pulled her riding boots onto her feet, and stood in her crêpe-de-Chine blouse and the covert-coating riding-breeches. Then came the coat and hat and gloves, and taking her hunting-crop she was complete.

But for quite five minutes she had not the pluck to go into the passage, and was standing there hesitating, when Bayard Delaval's deep voice could be heard calling from beneath the window:

"Are you ready, Miss Pelham? We ought to start."

So Nadine plucked up courage and boldly went down.

Sadie was already there, perfectly at home in her costume, as it was the natural American riding-dress. Eustace had just told her how charming she looked.

But when Nadine appeared he could not restrain an exclamation of surprise. She seemed the most delicious little figure and utterly unlike anything he had ever seen before.

Her black curls escaped from the soft felt hat in a way none of her family would have approved of.

If Sadie had not been in a similar costume, Eustace would have expressed his feelings to his fiancée. Bayard Delaval, on the contrary, found Nadine everything that was attractive.

She had not the slightest look of an English-woman; in fact she might have been some slender gipsy boy.

She was as light as a feather as he mounted her onto the back of one of the horses, and then he sprung into the saddle of another beside her.

Nadine, now thoroughly at home in her own

element, was as gay as a schoolboy. Anything to do
with horses came naturally to her.

She had quite determined that today she
meant to enjoy herself, cost what it might of her
father's anger. She meant to keep Mr. Delaval with
her and just let herself go.

Sadie and Eustace were mounted now and the
four started out of the camp in high spirits.

Nothing could surpass the wildness of the
country they rode through, which was full of sage
brush and huge rocky crags.

Sometimes one pair was ahead, and sometimes
the other, and now and then all four halted to gaze
at a view.

"It looks just the place for rattlesnakes," said
Sadie lightly. "I should not care to be walking off
the track."

The subject of rattlesnakes fascinated Nadine,
but somehow she had never thought of them as
realities.

"Are there really snakes here?" she asked
Bayard as they rode ahead.

"Quite a number of them. They are one of the
miner's curses when he is prospecting—I loathe
snakes."

"I had the strangest dream about them when
we were on the private car one afternoon. I had
never thought of them before in my life."

"What was it?" he asked with interest.

"I dreamt that there were a coil of them and
one came after me, and it sprung at me to bite, but
I thrust it from me and it slithered away. And after
it had gone I felt dreadfully sorry.

"Now, was not that perfectly silly, to have felt
sorry that a snake *hadn't* bitten one?"

81

"Yes, it is curious. I suppose your eye had seen a rattler from the train window, without consciously registering the fact.

"Our dreams are generally about something which has affected the subconscious mind during the day, but sometimes—very rarely—they seem to have some weird significance."

Then he told Nadine interesting stories of the mining camp. He was determined not to let himself get out of hand.

If at the end of the trip he saw plainly that the engagement of Eustace Pelham and Nadine was really as distasteful to them both as it appeared to be, then it might be a different thing.

But in any case, the life in a rough mining camp was not the kind of thing he would like to offer any girl, and his own life would lie here for the next year.

So the outlook in every way was not promising.

Perhaps that had something to do with the reserve which Nadine suddenly felt had fallen upon him.

She liked his appearance this morning. He wore miner's breeches, riding-boots with spurs, an open-necked silk shirt, a slouch felt hat, and a loose Norfolk jacket.

There was something picturesque and unconventional about this western dress, and it showed his lean, active figure.

Every moment Nadine was falling more in love with him.

Just before they reached the shaft of the mine, Eustace had the intelligence to come up and join them, and Bayard fell back to Sadie, so that when they came in sight of the two elderly gentlemen, the couples were assorted just as they should have been all the way.

Sir Edward remarked on this with pleasure, and felt glad that he had given Eustace a timely hint before breakfast.

He was absolutely horrified, however, when he saw his daughter's outfit, and Sadie, seeing a storm impending, took the bull by the horns.

"Now don't be cross, Sir Edward, at Nadine wearing my things. We never ride any other way out here, and they are perfect outfits to go down the mine in."

This was incontrovertible. So, Sir Edward was obliged to swallow his displeasure.

Lunch had been sent on for them, and they had the merriest meal, and then they put on canvas overalls and sou'westers, and were ready to go down the mine.

They went first in a sort of big bucket, four at a time, on a gradual slant downwards, and then they got out at a kind of stage, and Nadine and Sadie had to step onto a narrow board, with an iron support going up through the middle to a cross-bar at the top, which was attached to the support chains at the sides.

They clung to the iron centre-piece, and Mr. Delaval and a mine manager who had joined them stood beyond the girls, also holding on to the bar but with one arm tight round each girl's waist.

It is a very strange feeling to be standing clinging to an iron post on a board that was suspended in mid-air on loose chains, and both girls felt immensely excited.

Nadine, so close to Bayard in the pitch dark,

quivered in his arms, and he had to use the whole of his will not to bend his head and kiss her.

But fortunately the commonplace level was kept by Sadie's remarks and giggles. So at last they arrived six hundred feet below, and the cage went back up for the rest of the party.

And then Bayard Delaval took command.

Nadine hardly heard Bayard's explanations about high grade. She felt she wanted to slip her hand into his, and implore him to take her out of the mine and come with her to safety.

She controlled herself, but her heart was beating to suffocation, and at last, after hours it seemed, they were soon to be starting for the earth's surface again.

When the big bucket began to reach upper air, Nadine's spirits revived, but she was very pale.

"I hate your mine!" she said when they reached the top of the shaft and stood once more in the sunlight.

"Oh, how divine to breathe again." And before Sir Edward and Mr. Bronson and the managers and head officials could take off their overalls, the four young people had moved towards the horses again.

"Who'll race me back to the hotel?" Nadine cried, as Bayard mounted; and without waiting to see who would come with her, she galloped ahead.

Sadie did not too greatly encourage her horse to follow at that breakneck pace, and Eustace, who had mounted last, was obliged, not unwillingly, to stay with her!

Two hundred yards farther on Bayard Delaval caught up with Nadine.

All the Pan-spirit in her was in ascendance.
She was so thankful to have escaped some imagi-
nary danger.

She made her mount cavort and show some
life, and Bayard had to spur his horse to keep up
with her. He called to her, because without heed-
ing she had struck into the wrong track.

When he came alongside her, he put his hand
on the bridle.

"Did you want to run away from me, Miss
Pelham, alone into the wilds? You have taken the
wrong turn, you know."

"Have I?" She laughed. "How delightful! We
have been doing the right things in all those horrible hours down in your Hades. One could never be
really lost up here in the light."

"You don't want to turn back, then, and go
the way the others have gone?"

"Not I. I want to find a track for myself, even
if it penetrates into the unknown."

"Very well. It is not unknown to me, though.
It is a few miles out of the way, that is all. It comes
near to a shack I built last year, which I retire to
when I want to work out some mining problem
entirely alone.

"I don't believe another soul now knows of its
existence; the boys who helped me build it went
back East last fall."

"It must be wonderful to be quite alone out
here, with only Nature. I envy you."

"It is a pretty rough life, and not fit for your
dainty feet."

"It depends what one wants life to mean to
one," she said seriously.

85

"Have you any idea what that would be?"

He rode quite close to her and tried to look into her eyes, which were lowered.

"Vaguely. I would want it to mean that I meant the whole world to someone, not that I was just an ornament or a duty. I would like to give the 'broidered sleeve,' as the Lady of Frussasco gave Bayard in my book."

She had paused a little in the pronouncing of the name Bayard, and it thrilled him.

Then she asked him about his career, because she felt that they were getting on to too-dangerous ground.

The horses were going at walking pace now.

"I would like to be so rich that I could be quite free to give my whole brain to something higher than making money.

"Then I would like to think out, and then carry out, some scheme which would benefit and help numbers of people that I now see staggering under burdens, without the sense to get them off their backs themselves and with no one to show them how to do so."

Nadine was listening, profoundly interested.

His face was so strong and keen, and his clear eyes seemed to be looking ahead, always at something fine.

Oh, how wonderful it would be to help him to do great things, instead of having to follow a backboneless, uninterested Eustace!

This last thought came with such a stab that she suddenly spurred her horse, and it bounded ahead, the quick movement rousing her joyous spirit again.

She laughed back at Bayard!

She knew now that she would probably be scolded for riding on ahead with him, even if they got back to the hotel at the same time as the others.

Her sudden spring forward had left him time to think, and he knew he had better begin to put more control on his emotions, because he was utterly fascinated.

It was very difficult, though, to keep up a dignified reserve with a mischievous Nature sprite, which is what Nadine appeared as she looked back at him.

They heard the motors come along the main road and pass on, and Nadine laughed delightedly.

"Oh, how divine that we are not being chased by them! They will go on their good old stupid, respectable way, back to Blenkie!"

She made her horse bound forward again. Bayard's sense of exaltation and freedom rose too. It was all a joy, no matter what his good resolutions might be.

He came up beside her and put his hand on her reins, bringing the horses level.

The country was indescribably wild, with the huge boulders and rocky crags jutting out of sandy stony soil. Strange desert wild flowers of apricot and heliotrope colours seemed to spring from barren earth amidst the sage brush.

Not a bird was in the air; the late afternoon sun was growing lower and the shadows had become tinged with turquoise and violet.

It seemed as though they were alone together in some dominion of their own. When they came to a more open space, Bayard said:

"Let us dismount now for a few minutes; the horses cannot climb where I want to take you."

Nadine pulled in her reins, pleased to do anything which kept them away from the others a little longer.

She was experiencing such joy.

Some kind of wonderful moment seemed to be near. She analyzed nothing, but Nature was whispering to her that soon she must be in his arms, and let fathers, fiancés, and engagement rings rip!

But because her desire seemed so near, that contrariness in woman came uppermost, and she sprang lightly to the ground without waiting for him to help her. And while he tied the horses' bridles together, she climbed up a great stone.

He joined her, and soon they reached a canyon, where the most astonishing picture met their view.

They were on the very edge of a vast abyss that was unsuspected until the climb was made.

Forbidding crags clustered all round, and away across the colossal chasm the rocks looked the colour of purple hyacinths in the lowering light.

The sky was opal above them, turning to rose and gold towards the west. It was intensely hot and still.

The impossible seemed to have happened:

"The time, the place, and the loved one all together!"

Bayard came close to Nadine, leaning against the rock behind them. Every nerve in them both quivered with the force of awakening love.

"Here we are," he whispered, "like eagles in an aerie, and this desert is our Garden of Eden;

for now there are no other people but just our own two selves in all the world."

She turned her face towards him, and he saw the passion in her eyes.

She was his mate. Surely she loved him, and he who knew all about passion and the delirium of it could teach her to know every joy.

He loved her. Who should dare to come between them? No parent, no laggard-in-love!

They belonged to each other. Two fierce, primitive-natured people who would understand the same things.

His hesitation was gone now. Love was the arbiter; there was no more question of a fair game. If Eustace meant nothing to her, why should she remain tied to him? That was an unfair game.

He put out his strong hand and touched her gloved one.

"Nadine, I love you," he cried, and had just begun to take her in his arms.

A hundred yards down in the open space, the two quiet horses waited patiently.

But what was that stealthy, sinuous, glistening thing which suddenly began gliding towards them from the sage brush!

Their eyes started from their heads in terror, and with wild snorts they broke away and galloped towards the path!

Nadine felt that everything in her was melting and that her whole being was merged with Bayard's. But before she could answer him or his lips meet hers in a kiss, they both heard the horses move, and, startled, they stood upright.

Bayard knew that the situation brooked no

89

delay. He released Nadine and bounded down the crags in a vain attempt to head the animals at the turn, and as he crossed the sage brush, unseen by either of them, the great snake struck out at him, but he had passed beyond its range.

The seriousness of what was happening did not present itself to Nadine. She was annoyed that anything should have interrupted the divinest moment of her life, but this was only another phase of the perfect day's adventure, and she prepared to descend and help in the chase.

The snake was coiled again, its cunning head raised, alert.

Nadine had taken off one of her gloves, in her agitation, and now she paused for a moment, because Bayard was calling to her:

"They have gone past the turn. We will never catch them now! It looks like a long hike for us."

He started to come back to her.

She laughed gaily and waved her glove at him, never seeing that the snake was near, ready to strike.

The glove slipped out of her hand, and fell sharply against the great coiled reptile at her feet.

With eyes still fixed upon Bayard, she bent to pick it up, when, with a hideous rattle, the serpent raised itself and buried its fangs in her left shoulder, and the poison entered her blood.

She started back with an agonized shriek, and the snake, having spent its venom, undulated away among the grey rocks before Bayard could reach the spot.

Horror convulsed him when he realized what had occurred, and he covered the ground between them with giant strides. Nadine was in an agony of terror and pain.

She vaguely knew that soon she might have to die, and life was very sweet. But Bayard Delaval never lost his head.

He put his arms round her, tore off her coat and then the sleeve from her blouse, and there were the two ominous purple marks.

The place had not yet had time to swell. Not a moment was to be lost.

While he held the terrified girl firmly with one arm, to prevent her from struggling, he found his knife with the other hand, and opened it with his teeth.

Her agonized eyes watched him. When she saw what he meant to do, she screamed, and unconsciously struggled frantically to get free.

She was down to primitive instincts now, all civilized training having fallen from her in her fear. She would have bitten him if she could.

He held her arms still, as in a vise, and, with what tenderness the desperate situation permitted, he cut into her shrinking olive-ivory flesh, and when the blood spurted he sucked the ugly wound to draw the poison out.

But by then, after one sobbing sigh of anguish, Nadine had fainted, and now she lay limp in his encircling arms.

Her hat fell from her head, and her short curls, released from most of their few pins, tumbled in a thick mass over his coat sleeve.

With a cry of grief and misery, Bayard held her passionately to his heart.

❊   ❊   ❊

At seven o'clock Sadie Bronson and Eustace rode up to the hotel door at Gold Rock, without the other two young people.

Sir Edward, who had arrived half an hour before, and who was smoking on the veranda with Mr. Bronson and some of the mine officials, rose and came towards them.

He was annoyed. This was not a suitable pairing of the quartette, and Eustace had no right to have allowed it to occur.

Sadie, as usual, smoothed the situation.

"We were racing back, and Nadine was ahead, but she must have taken the wrong turn, Sir Edward, because Mr. Delaval tore after her ... I suppose to point it out to her ... and we missed them.

"We thought we would find them here before us."

Sir Edward could not express his displeasure in words, but Eustace felt that he was very angry; and, like all weak-natured people, knowing himself to be in the wrong, he blamed others.

"Nadine would not keep alongside any of us," he said shortly. "To go as fast as she could was all that concerned her."

Then, having assisted Sadie to dismount, he entered the hotel and went up to his room to change.

Sadie was radiant. She had "brought Eustace along," as she expressed it to herself, and had made him feel that she was the only companion who would not bore him.

The flirtation was no longer tentative but a clear fact. She stayed on the veranda, saying delightful things to the irate parent of Nadine, until she had soothed him.

"They'll be here in a minute, of course. Nothing could happen to them, and Mr. Delaval knows the way."

Half an hour passed, Sadie keeping the conversation even, and then she went into the hotel.

"I suppose we'll have supper about eight-thirty," she said, kissing her hand to her father.

Quarter to nine came before she descended again, and the party were assembled waiting on the veranda, very hungry and impatient.

The culprits had not yet put in an appearance. Sir Edward was now very anxious.

He knew that Nadine's awe of him would never have allowed her to stay behind deliberately like this. Something must have happened to them.

"Should we go and look for them?" Eustace suggested half-heartedly.

He was convinced that no matter what had occurred, Bayard Delaval was quite capable of taking care of a woman, and he had a shrewd suspicion that Nadine would enjoy an adventure with him!

As they all stood there peering into the darkness which comes so suddenly in those western climes, the sound of horses trotting could be heard in the distance, and the tension upon Sir Edward's face relaxed a little.

Yes, two horses were approaching; but as the tired animals passed the veranda, the lights from the windows showed that they were riderless.

The men made a rush across the dusty ground just as the man who attended to them caught their dragging and broken bridles.

No, there were no marks of an accident, the horses had not fallen.

93

Everything pointed to the riders having dismounted, and that then the horses had broken away.

"Guess they've stopped off to look at the sunset," one engineer laughed, "and it'll be a long hike back."

Anger now had quenched anxiety in Sir Edward, and even Eustace felt aggrieved.

His fiancée had no business to take interest in sunsets, and it was most unladylike to make scandals in this way.

"If you think they are walking, we will go to meet them," Sir Edward announced in a frigid voice.

And as quickly as possible two motors were brought round. Sir Edward's face was set as if in a mask of stone.

He was too reserved a person to vent his fury upon Eustace, whom he felt was partly to blame, because if he had shown proper attention to his fiancée she would not have had the opportunity to dismount with the attractive young mining engineer!

So both men remained in grim silence, feeling that some climax must occur.

Unless Nadine had the most perfectly proper explanation to offer, Eustace felt that his dignity would not permit him to go on with their engagement.

He did not analyze his motives, or he would have discovered that inclination would prompt him to catch at any straw to be free.

Sir Edward was saying to himself that from now on, until her marriage, Nadine should not leave his or Miss Blenkensop's side, and that the

94

marriage should take place the moment they returned to England, which would be within a month.

They drove back all the weary miles to the mine.

Not a trace of the pair could they find. The sleepy watchmen had seen nothing and heard nothing. So at about midnight they turned back again, Sir Edward a prey to alternate anger and fear.

When they got to the hotel once more, the other motor had also returned, after a fruitless search.

Almost wild with anxiety now, Sir Edward insisted upon starting out again. There must be some branch-paths, and they would follow every one.

Eustace's ill-temper increased with every mile. He now felt that he hated Nadine.

They reached the mine the second time, just after three o'clock. Another watchman suggested that about a mile down the track there was a turn-off concealed by a great rock, which they would not be likely to notice in the dark, but which led to a bridle-path which eventually got back to the camp.

So the two weary men entered the motor once more, and drove very slowly, examining every yard of the way. They were too anxious to remember how hungry they were!

At last, after carefully searching, they came to what appeared to be the turning, and they went along it on an impossible road.

After about half an hour's creeping over stones and in ruts, just when the eastern sky had begun to change, Sir Edward, peering from one side, called a halt.

There was a light not very far away up the mountainside. Could they be there? But in any case, perhaps some information might be obtained about them.

Both men got out quickly, and told the driver to wait for them there.

But what was that sound which suddenly met their ears, floating across to them in the still air? Surely it was . . . weird Russian music?

Sir Edward held his breath, for now he could distinguish the tune.

Someone, or a gramophone, was playing the "Red Sarafane."

"My God! Eustace, do you hear that?" he said in a broken voice. "Come on."

*　　*　　*

Was she going to die, this beloved creature, just when it seemed that their love would burst all bonds and declare itself?

No, not if human resources and will could save her.

Bayard looked about wildly for a second, but he knew that no help would come from outside. It was a million to one that anyone would ever pass that way by chance.

There to the north, farther up the mountain, on the other side of the path, his little shack could just be seen.

He lifted his unconscious burden—she seemed as light as a baby to the big, strong man—and soon he was striding up the hill with her, and at last he reached the shanty and pushed open the door.

It was just a boarded room, with an old wooden bed in one corner, covered with dark-looking blankets.

Bayard put his precious bundle tenderly down on the bed, then rapidly went to the cupboard and got out a glass and a bottle of whisky, real scotch, in spite of Prohibition!

The bottle was about three-parts full. He filled the tumbler to the brim and took it over to the bed.

Nadine lay dead as a log. He raised her in his arms gently and forced the glass between her lips.

It almost seemed that his touch revived her, for her eyes opened for a moment, and he poured some of the spirits down her throat.

The choking completely awoke her.

"You must drink this," he said sternly.

The danger to her permitted no delay for persuasion. The gipsy half of Nadine was the only part of her spirit which seemed conscious, and it immediately recognized a master; she swallowed the whisky in gulps.

If she hesitated for a moment, Bayard spoke again with a tone of firm authority. He did not stop until she had taken the whole big tumblerful.

Then he let her lie back on the pillow, and he covered her up with the coarse brown blankets.

If he had been in time, he believed, she would now be saved, for the great quantity of whisky would counteract the poison, as every miner knew.

But had he been in time?

Nadine seemed to fall into a semi-conscious stupor, but when he felt her pulse, her heart was beating a little more strongly than before. So he

97

could leave her for a moment, to prepare to wash the wound.

He poured more of the whisky into some water, and then very tenderly bathed the wound, putting on as well as he could a bandage made of a turned-up handkerchief.

She let him do as he liked, with her eyes half-closed and breathing heavily.

Then, when the bandaging was finished, he settled her once more on the bed. And now she seemed to fall into a drugged sleep.

By this time the sun had set and the short twilight of rosy crimson pervaded the room.

Bayard sat down and watched. Nadine began to toss restlessly, and darkness fell upon the place.

He got up, lit the lamp, and wound up the cheap clock on the table by his watch. It was eight o'clock.

By now, Sir Edward and the rest would have begun to wonder what could have become of them.

He went back to the bed. The strain he had suffered was telling a little, and he felt tired now that his anxiety had lessened.

A sip of whisky would have been a very nice thing, but he knew that he must not waste a drop of it. She would have to have some more, if this amount did not produce a lasting effect.

He was hungry, too. But he had often been in situations of real hardship, and it never even entered his head that he needed anything himself.

His whole mind was fixed upon the sleeping girl.

One crisp black curl lay over the pillow, and he touched it reverently with his fingers. Even in her heavy sleep she seemed conscious of his nearness, as a half-smile stole over her lips for an instant.

He had a strong desire to lift her into his arms and let her sleep on his breast, or rock and soothe her like a baby, but some chivalrous instinct made him feel that he must not take the least advantage of the situation to gratify any of his own desires.

So, hour after hour she slept on, moaning sometimes, and from time to time he wet the bandage on her shoulder. Then he would stretch himself and go to the door to look out.

He did not draw the cheap, checked cotton curtains over the two windows; better that the light should be seen, if by some fortunate chance help should come.

Not a sound could be heard, except an occasional faint rustle as a reptile or lizard passed among the brush.

The stars were very bright, and a crescent waning moon had just risen in the east.

The clock struck half-past two. Nadine had been sleeping more peacefully for the last quarter of an hour, and Bayard sat down in the chair by the writing-table and rested his head in his hands.

He had almost slipped into the unconsciousness of sleep for a second, when he was aroused by a movement on the bed.

Was Nadine awakening?

He went to her, but by then she had sunk back again.

All the top of her sleeve was wrenched away, and her blouse was very disordered, but there were hardly any blood marks.

Her round young throat gleamed ivory against the dark holland pillow. The fine lace and the pale pink crêpe-de-Chine of her petticoat just showed where the blouse had been torn open, and all her beautiful neck was bare.

A bright flush was in her cheeks now. Even in this unnatural sleep she was utterly attractive to the young mining engineer.

He sat down beside her and now began to think clearly.

What would this sinister adventure mean in the workings of Fate?

Would it draw them nearer, or would it part them? How he loved her! He realized the magnitude of his passion from the agony which came to him with the thought that she might die.

"My darling, my little girl," he murmured over and over again.

What did she really feel for him beyond the physical attraction which he knew united them both?

She knew nothing of his status in life. For her, he was probably just someone whom she was attracted by, but of whose worldly position she had taken no account, not even thinking of him as a possible husband.

He understood that her upbringing, and the European point of view, would certainly make her consider a mining engineer as of a different rank from her own, so it would be love alone which would make her give herself to him.

This was a glorious thought.

He would never let her know that he had a fortune and breeding behind him, until she was really his own, if he could help it.

Sir Edward would make an awful fuss and

certainly would refuse his consent. They would have to have a runaway marriage.

Then he would take her down to his old Virginia home, and give her a surprise; something of its old-world atmosphere and state would remind her of England.

And how his father and his widowed aunt, who lived there with him, would rejoice! And all the dear servants would adore her.

The whole family had longed for him to marry since he turned twenty-five

His thoughts ran on, each one thrilling him. Then the clock struck three, and as though the sound had awakened her, Nadine started into a sitting position.

It would be safest to give her more whisky, Bayard felt.

So he poured more into the tumbler, and now, with what he had used to bathe her shoulder, the bottle was empty.

She was gazing about her in a dazed way, and shrinking every other moment with the pain.

He came over to her with the half-filled glass. "You must drink some more," he said.

She took it obediently and swallowed about a third, then pushed it from her.

"Now you must lie down again," he commanded, and she sank back and closed her eyes.

He covered her up, fearing to speak in case he should rouse her completely, so he took the chair by the writing-table again.

He felt that he could not look at her, for the temptation to take her in his arms was so great.

Half an hour passed.

101

Then suddenly Nadine sat up.

He went to her at once, and made his voice stern as he said:

"You must lie down."

She gave a little whimper, as would a child in distress, and then she snuggled into the blankets.

He sat beside her on the bed and covered her up once more. She shut her eyes, but he remained sitting there for a moment, to see what she would do.

Then her little hand stole up and caressed his face, which was leaning above her.

Her touch made him quiver.

He put her hand back again under the blankets.

"You must go to sleep," he said. "Do you hear, Miss Pelham?"

Now her face filled with mischief, and she seemed to have forgotten the pain in her shoulder. She was lying there, pouting and looking up at him out of half-shut, alluring blue eyes.

"Bayard," she lisped. "Miss Pelham, indeed! I am Nadine, and you are my lover."

The first tumbler of whisky had killed the poison and saved her life. Could this last small quantity have intoxicated her a little? Bayard wondered.

It was not normal to act that way after a severe snake bite, but . . .

And then suddenly he realized that, at all events, all inhibitions were numbed in her brain, and the real Nadine was gazing at him with soft, voluptuous eyes.

In vino veritas.

Every vestige of the civilized English girl seemed to fall from her as she looked up at him.

She was the wild Russian gipsy, with every art to entice a man to heaven or hell at her fingertips.

"I must sit up," she said. "Bayard, why won't you let me?"

She struggled into a sitting position.

"I want to stretch."

Short of holding her in bed by force, he could not now prevent her from rising, and he was afraid of the temptations if he should touch her.

She put her feet to the ground.

"You see, I am all right." She held out her arms to him. "I thought you loved me. Don't you?"

He came over to her.

"My God! You know I do. But you have been awfully ill, which is why you must rest."

"I won't rest . . . without you."

She caught hold of his shirt-sleeve and rubbed her cheek up and down it. He had taken off his coat to make an extra cover for her feet when he had first laid her down.

She was utterly provoking. No caressing tricks that he could imagine seemed to be unknown to her, and her eyes were temptation itself, magnetizing him with their voluptuous passion.

"You must lift me, Bayard, I want to be in your arms."

He controlled his rising emotion, and picked her up and laid her on the bed again.

There were apparently no pins in her hair at all now, and it fell just to her neck in thick black curls.

The bright but pale scarlet flush was in her

103

cheeks, and her lips were very red and pursed up as though asking for kisses.

Bayard tried to be matter-of-fact.

He went and got the basin of whisky and water again, to moisten the bandage once more.

She kept laughing at him, and when he tried to put it on, she turned and kissed his fingers, and bit one of them gently, like a little animal at play.

Bayard's pulses were bounding. How was he going to resist this adorable thing?

"Bayard . . . my knight who has come to set me free," she whispered, as though repeating something she had learned.

"I could see you out the window, and I knew at once you were my lover and my lord. Why did you not stay that day instead of Eustace? But you will never leave me now . . . never again, will you? Promise me."

"Of course not," he said hoarsely, at his wits' end, because her hands were again caressing his face.

"You are my lover, Bayard. Why are you so cold?"

"I'm not cold. Only you don't know how ill you have been. The snake bit your shoulder."

"Oh, what do I care for snakes! I am here alone with you, and I am going to stay with you always, away from the silly old world. Bayard, tell me you love me."

All the deep-down, primitive instincts, which had been suppressed all her life, were now stirring in Nadine.

She was conscious of nothing but that she was with the man she loved.

Bayard was going through torture. How was he to keep from responding to her?

He had studied the workings of the subconscious mind, and he believed that Nadine was now letting him see her real feelings, whether she was intoxicated or not.

Her voice was not the least thick, nor were there any of the usual signs of having taken too much whisky.

"Nadine," he said gravely, unclasping her two hands, which were clinging to his neck, "won't you rest just while look I out and see if they are coming to find us?"

But this roused fierce resentment.

"They shall not come! I am yours, and I will stay with you . . . forever."

Ah! If this could only be so. If he could only take her away with him for his very own, now, without delay.

Her words awakened passionate thoughts. He too was having primitive instincts aroused.

But she was alone with him, entirely at his mercy, and perhaps she was not quite mistress of herself. He must not take the least advantage of her.

"Nadine—sweetheart," he whispered in a choked voice. "Tomorrow we will arrange everything, but tonight you must lie still and rest. Don't you know, a snake's bite is a dangerous thing, and I must take care of you."

She put her hand up vaguely to her shoulder.

"It's hot," she said, "but it does not hurt. Bayard, why don't you take me in your arms and hold me where I want to be . . . my lover . . . ?"

The young man was almost beside himself. She looked indescribably alluring, her blue eyes, as bright as stars, gleaming at him, with a world of passion in them, from between her forest of black lashes.

He crushed his emotions, soothed and coaxed her, and got her to lie down at last.

Then he left the shack and went out into the night. It had begun to lighten in the east, for it was nearly four o'clock.

His heart was beating fast and his head was swimming. Not a sound could be heard.

No, they would have to stay there until the morning, and this agonizing temptation would go on. How was he going to be able to be the Knight Bayard through the hours?

While he leaned against the corner of a wall, of the shack, peering towards the only direction from which anyone could approach, he might have heard in the distance a motor stop, but his ears were startled by the Victrola inside.

Nadine must have set it in motion. It was playing a new record he had brought back from Europe with him, a Russian arrangement of the old national air, the "Red Sarafane."

He turned back quickly, and as he entered the shack he stopped in the doorway, and stood still, in admiration.

For it seemed as if a Russian gipsy was dancing there! Round and round the little figure flew, with all the stamping, fluttering, wildly voluptuous movements which only the gipsies knew.

Bayard had seen the Russian ballet and various troupes of dancers at revues, so he recognized the origin of the thing.

He realized that it must be heredity showing. The Russian half of Nadine's nature was coming into its own.

He fell entirely under the spell of her strange blue eyes, which were looking at him with sensuous passion. They were leading him—where?

She came closer and closer each time she passed, until at last she flung herself into his arms. Bayard was a strong man, and chivalrous, but he was passionately in love.

He put the sternest restraint upon himself once more, and carried her to the bed. She was exhausted by this time and should certainly rest.

She seemed to be quite docile, content that his arms held her, but when he laid her down, with one of her sudden movements she put both arms round his neck and, raising herself, pressed her soft young lips to his.

Then madness seized him, and for one brief moment he lost control of himself and let the wild passion he was feeling return her kiss.

Oh, the delirious joy of it! Time and place seemed to be swept away, drowned in the exquisite bliss of their first embrace!

The scratching of the Victrola needle coincided with the opening of the cabin door, and Sir Edward, white as death, strode towards them, followed by Eustace.

Fate seemed to be closing in upon them with a heavy hand! . . .

Chapter
Five

When the two men had reached the cabin, Sir Edward, motioning Eustace aside, went forward alone to look in through the window.

And the sight which met his view was certainly calculated to arouse the worst suspicions!

From there he saw his daughter reclining on the bed, clasped in the arms of the young mining engineer, her hair dishevelled and her blouse torn, while their lips were meeting in a passionate kiss.

"My God! The disgrace has come at last!" he whispered brokenly, and, followed by Eustace, he pushed open the door and entered the room.

In all the future years of his life, no moment would ever be quite so awful to Bayard Delaval as was this one, when, while his lips still met the passionate young lips of Nadine, he became aware of her father's entrance.

Here he was, discovered in a completely false position, which he felt no words could explain away.

He cursed his weakness. How far short he had fallen from the ideal Knight Bayard! Why—why had he given way, even for that one brief instant!

He rose, drew himself to his full height, and faced the two men squarely.

Nadine, defiant, only angry at this interruption to her joy, still clung to him, having bounded from the bed when Bayard left her, on her father's entrance.

"I could kill you both," Sir Edward said in a voice almost inaudible from pain and shame.

"You are doing your daughter and me an injustice, Sir," Bayard Delaval said. "She was bitten by a rattlesnake, and . . ."

Sir Edward interrupted him, shaking his stick.

"Far better, then, that it had killed her than that the Pelham name should suffer this everlasting disgrace."

Bayard winced as if at a blow; then Nadine broke in:

"How dare you speak so to my lover, Papa! I love him, I want to stay in his arms and never leave him again. He is my Knight Bayard, come to set me free. Go away, you wicked man. I hate you. Leave us alone!"

Here Eustace broke in, in a tone of withering contempt:

"There seems to be only one thing that the 'Knight Bayard' can do then, and that is to marry the lady with the least possible delay."

"I am ready and proud to do so immediately, Sir, and give you and her father what satisfaction you may desire afterwards."

Bayard's eyes flashed grey fire while he circled Nadine with his arm.

"Do you hear, Papa? We are going to be married now."

"Very well. It is the best thing which can happen to you. You shall come straight back to the Justice of the Peace this minute, and he will marry you at dawn.

"And as for satisfaction, all that I ask of you, Sir, is that you take my daughter and that I never see either of you again."

"Sir Edward, you are making a frightful mistake, I warn you," Bayard answered quietly. "Will you not let me explain? Your daughter has done no wrong, but I am only too happy to marry her, if she will have me for her husband. Will you, Nadine?"

Nadine clung to his arm.

"Of course I will. Now . . ."

Sir Edward came close to her, and took her left hand, from which he drew the engagement ring, and then he handed it back to Eustace.

"You *must* listen to me," Bayard said sternly. "Your daughter is ill and in pain . . ." And then his voice faltered for a moment.

How was he to explain away the scene that the two men must have witnessed? He could not tell them of the long hours of temptation. Nor that at last she had put her lips to his.

How would they believe that she was suffering, when they had heard the Victrola, and for all he could tell had seen her dancing like a mad thing, and then there were her own words, spoken wildly, that he was her lover.

"I tell you, you have misunderstood everything, Sir Edward," he said again. "Can you not see for yourself the wound in Miss Pelham's shoulder? The rattlesnake bit her, and it is only a

111

miracle that she is not dead. Her blouse is torn because I cut the place with my knife. That, and the whisky, saved her life."

At this Eustace made a slight exclamation, as though light might be dawning in his mind. He glanced again at the empty bottle, which he had noticed when he entered, but Sir Edward drew back with freezing hauteur.

"I do not require any explanation, Sir. I am not questioning as to whether the snake bit her or did not bite her, whether you tore her blouse or cut her shoulder, or gave her whisky, or saved her life.

"I request you to marry my daughter *on the evidence of my own eyes*, which saw her lying in your arms in a passionate embrace. She is a girl, and a gentlewoman, and furthermore she is engaged to another man!"

During this speech Nadine had been rubbing her cheek up and down Bayard's shirt-sleeve again, evincing adoring little tricks of fondness for him, her naughty, flushed, lovely face full of passionate love.

"Come," said her father, with icy sternness, to hide the agony he was suffering, for he could see Nada standing there, behaving in the very same way.

"You can keep your caresses for when you are alone with your husband. The Justice of the Peace will, no doubt, be about when we get back, so you will not have to wait long!"

"So be it," Bayard said hoarsely. "But one day you will right this shameful wrong that you are committing against your own child. For my

112

part, I am proud and happy, for I love her, and will protect her with my life."

He took his coat off the bed and wrapped it round Nadine, as her own was somewhere out on the hill.

Then he lifted her tenderly into his arms to carry her to the waiting automobile, and as he did so, the last hairpin fell out of her hair and onto the table by the door.

He set her down for a second, put it in his pocket, then picked her up again and strode on.

The party set out in the dawn down the rough craggy hill, and reached the motor in silence.

Nadine was not conscious of what was happening when they arrived at the Office of the Justice of the Peace, everything seemed as if it were a dream.

And when Bayard asked her to go into the inner room, she rose obediently and followed them, still wearing his coat, so that the wound in her shoulder would not be seen.

All she registered for the moment was a confused murmur of voices, and that she was being told to repeat some words which had no meaning to her; and then Bayard was taking her hand and putting a bit of wire round her finger, a hairpin that he had twisted into a ring.

Then they were in the automobile again, and so to the hotel; and there was Blenkie, as white as a ghost, still on the veranda, waiting, with her knitting in a hopeless tangle in her hands.

"She has been bitten by a rattlesnake, Miss Blenkensop," Bayard said to the terrified governess. "I will go for the doctor at once. Take care of her, and put her to bed!"

The events of the night and everything had become a blank to Nadine, who collapsed into unconsciousness.

In the dingy bedroom, Blenkie undressed the unconscious girl as best she could, and there Nadine lay in bed, with eyes closed, half-asleep and half-unconscious.

Underneath, in her refrigerated heart, Miss Blenkensop loved her pupil, as indeed did everyone who knew her well.

Her pixie pranks might irritate, but her warm, generous heart always showed in the long run. Blenkie was going through miserable anxiety until the doctor came.

"Here is Dr. Heathcott to see Mrs. Delaval," Bayard said, entering the room with him.

Miss Blenkensop actually jumped.

"*Mrs.* Delaval!" she cried, aghast. Then she swallowed rapidly several times.

Sitting by the bed and watching Nadine, she had noticed the bit of twisted wire round the third finger of her left hand, and had wondered vaguely what caprice was this, and what had become of her engagement ring.

But Blenkie was not a person to ask questions. All she blurted out was:

"Does Sir Edward know?"

Bayard nodded; then, after making a sign to the doctor that he would wait in the passage, he left the room.

The doctor examined the wound and then sent Blenkie for water and a basin; he had heard from Bayard all the details of how and when the bite had occurred and the remedies which had been applied.

"She's out of danger," he announced, having given her some drops from a phial. "The whisky saved her, but she's had a close call.

"She'll sleep now, maybe for twenty-four hours, waking and slipping off again perhaps. But she won't be herself or understand anything for quite that time. Let her have milk if she calls for anything."

At that moment Mrs. O'Hara came up the stairs with a message from Sir Edward.

Miss Blenkensop was to pack up and join the party below, which would start for Gold Stamp as soon as she could be ready.

Blenkie stood up stiffly, and flatly refused to go. Now that it came to the point, all her real affection for Nadine broke the bonds of restraint.

She could not leave Nadine alone while she was ill, and unconscious of what was going on.

"I shall stay, Mr. Delaval, no matter what Sir Edward says. I cannot leave the child."

Then Bayard came forward and took her hand.

"You are a gem, Miss Blenkensop, but if you stay it will only cause complications. Nadine will be all right now. I will take the tenderest care of her, and soon she can get her maid. But I am really grateful to you, and so will she be."

Sir Edward's voice was heard from the passage:

"Miss Blenkensop!"

As Bayard held open the door for her, Sir Edward came up the stairs, and Blenkie went on to pack.

Bayard stepped forward into the passage to meet his father-in-law.

"Sir Edward," he said, "the doctor says your daughter is now out of danger. Won't you let me explain everything to you before you go away?"

Sir Edward's face was white and set.

"I will make ample provision for *your wife*, Mr. Delaval. Her maid and luggage will await her at Gold Stamp, but I have no *daughter* now. Good day." And with that he walked away.

Bayard straightened himself and went back into Nadine's room.

And presently he heard the noise of the motor leaving, and he knew that she was utterly alone with him—his very own.

He came over nearer to the bed.

"My darling little wife," he murmured, and then he said a silent prayer.

Then, as there appeared no prospect of her waking for hours, he went off to snatch a bath in the men's dressing-shed and get some breakfast, locking the door after him.

And so began their wedding day.

When Bayard returned to his wife's room he was struck afresh by the appalling squalor of it.

It was all very well for one night, but to have to spend weeks here, or indeed two or three months, would be quite another matter.

He would have to settle all the work he could this afternoon, and then get away in the morning when she would wake.

He would take her back to Gold Stamp, to the hotel there, where at least she could have proper baths and food.

But then a blankness came over him. It would

be absolutely impossible for him to stay at Gold
Stamp because his place was at the mine; and Nadine was not the type to live in a hotel alone.

He almost wished now that he had arranged
with Miss Blenkensop to wait for them at Gold
Stamp. The situation was very difficult.

He stood looking at her from the foot of the
bed. She was exquisitely beautiful, he thought.

"As helpless as a baby," Bayard whispered to
himself, with moisture in his keen grey eyes.

"My little darling sweetheart wife."

He bent to kiss her gently, and then he drew
back—no—not a single caress. He must remember
to restrain himself.

Who could he trust to stay with her? There
were no women whom he knew in the camp. There
might have been a few miners' wives, but he knew
nothing of their character, and the rest of the
females were not of a type to be in Nadine's
presence.

Mrs. O'Hara? She would promise to stay and
watch, but would she keep her word? There was
nobody but "Uncle Frederick."

Here was an idea!

Uncle Frederick was a weird, crippled old man
who had been a miner in his day but now sold
from a pack buttons and thread and such-like, for
which he journeyed backwards and forwards to
Gold Stamp to procure.

He was kindly and good-natured, and devoted
to Bayard by ties of gratitude and affection.

If he had come in, as was his custom, on a
Thursday, he would be the only trustworthy person
to instal as nurse.

Bayard bent over her once more; yes, she was

sleeping soundly. Then he straightened himself abruptly, controlling temptation, and left the room, locking the door behind him.

Uncle Frederick was found in his accustomed place on the veranda, and told briefly what was required of him.

The old fellow's kindly blue eyes softened.

"Why, certainly, mate," he said, and followed Bayard into the room.

"Well, ain't she a peach!" he exclaimed when he caught sight of Nadine. "Guess that rattler knew what he was about! I'll sit as quiet as an owl until you come back." And he chuckled affectionately.

* * *

The news had gone round that "the Prince" was married. Married to that dandy daisy daughter of one of the bosses of the mine.

The suddenness of the ceremony seemed nothing remarkable to them, for they were accustomed to rough-and-tumble ways and rapid action.

Bayard had to stand some rather ribald chaff, but not too much of it, because he was held in awe!

But in spite of all the troubles which seemed to be going to raise complications in the immediate future, there would be some divine hours of happiness first.

How they would talk over their absurd wedding, and the hairpin wedding ring! The new one which he would replace it with should be a narrow band of sapphires as blue as her eyes.

How docile she had been when he had put the twisted wire on her finger! Perhaps it was the

118

solemnity of the vows they were making which had made her so quiet all the time.

When things could be settled up and he could spend weeks with her, what wonderful discoveries each would make!

So, all the way back to the shanty hotel, Bayard allowed himself to make plans and to dream of divine things!

He would talk over possibilities with her and see what could be done about her residence. The best of the summer was before them, although it would become very hot in July and August, and that was an extra difficulty.

By the winter he would somehow arrange to get a month or two off, and take her to Virginia; and by next year he would have realized his fortune sufficiently to put in a deputy, and have to come to Nevada only occasionally, to supervise things.

His thoughts kept saying:

"She loves me, she loves me as much as I love her!"

There was a great crowd of miners on the veranda. He got through them and their greetings as quickly as he could, and bounded up the stairs.

At the door of Nadine's room he came upon Mrs. O'Hara, with some of his clothes over her shoulder and his case in her hand.

"We can't give you a second room, Mr. Delaval, since this posse has come from Rockers Point. But 'tain't likely you'd be wantin' it now that you're married, I says to myself, so I'm just movin' your things!"

"I *must* keep my room, Mrs. O'Hara!"

She burst into a peal of laughter.

"You can't put over a stunt of that sort with

119

me, my boy! Two rooms for a honeymoon! Go on!"

Accustomed as Bayard was to the outspoken desert ways, and to Mrs. O'Hara's type of wit, he grew angry. This was a fresh and impossible complication.

"I tell you I must keep my room. Mrs. Delaval is ill and cannot be disturbed."

The hostess rocked with laughter.

"You should worry!" she gurgled. "Married this morning and two rooms tonight!"

She put down the case and the clothes and waddled off to the stairs, firing a parting shot over her shoulder:

"Bob Larkin's snoring in your bed now, dead to the world! And Billy Bounker's going to join him on the floor! Feel inclined to clear them, and make a fight . . . say?"

Quivering with anger, but routed, Bayard tapped gently at his wife's door—a fight could not be contemplated with Nadine there ill—and in a minute it was opened by old Uncle Frederick, with his finger on his lips.

"She seemed to rouse half an hour ago, and I gave her milk and tucked her up, and made her comfortable again, but she never knowed where she was, nor saw me, and she's off sound now. Guess she'll sleep till dawn."

Bayard carried in his things and put them in a heap in the corner, then drew Uncle Frederick into the passage.

"Just wait until I've bolted some supper, then I won't have to go out again."

The old man nodded and went back into the room.

Could anything be more annoying than this!

120

Bayard's face was like an iron mask as he ate his supper, and no one dared address a word to him.

Then he went outside and looked at the stars for a little, to steady himself.

He would require all his will, he knew! Old Uncle Frederick was nodding when Bayard got back to the room, and was glad to be relieved of his long vigil.

They wrung each other's hand, and then Bayard and his bride were left alone.

He turned the rocking chair so he would not be able to see her, to lessen temptation.

He made a bundle of his coat for a pillow, and lit a candle; he had bought two or three of them at the store, and he divided them into sections so that they would last all night.

So began the wedding night of Bayard and Nadine!

＊　　＊　　＊

Bayard Delaval steadily read the *Story of Bayard*, the knight, as he kept vigil.

And he smiled, but the nobleness of Bayard's character affected him; indeed, he was one who had made honour famous and a splendour to be striven for, "without fear and without reproach!"

He, this modern Bayard, was perhaps without fear, but he certainly could not claim to be without reproach in the past!

The simple story touched him profoundly, as all great things must touch fine souls, and it helped him to keep his vow through the hours.

He could not sleep, however, nor eliminate all passionate thoughts; he could only force his will to be obeyed.

Nadine turned once or twice, and he rose to see if she was waking. But no, the drug the doctor had given must have been a very strong one.

Suddenly, at about two o'clock, she began to talk in her sleep, incoherent rushes of words for the most part, from which now and then a clear sentence would emerge.

"Winnie, he's my Knight Bayard, come to set me free! I know I shall love him. . . . 'Eustace,' do I like the name 'Eustace'? . . . Not much!

"But what's in a name, Winnie! We can call him Bayard, if we please!"

A light dawned upon Bayard Delaval. She had seen him from the window that day and evidently thought that he was Eustace, whom she must have been expecting; that had been the reason for her emotion when first he had told her his name was Bayard!

And then a wave of joy and triumph came over him. So he had been her very first ideal! His was the image which had filled her imagination before she had become engaged to her cousin!

In all reasonable probability, he, Bayard, was her first love!

"And I shall be her only one, so help me, God!" he swore. "If a man can hold a woman, I shall hold Nadine!"

He went back to his rocking chair then, very happy, and soon he too fell asleep, for he was worn out.

He was awakened at four o'clock by a tap on the door. It was old Uncle Frederick, come to tell him that there had been a fight between some of the watchmen at the mine and some newcomers, and he must come at once and settle things.

The old man promised to stay in the passage and let no one enter the room.

Bayard tore off to the automobile which was waiting with the messenger who had brought the news. Bitter disappointment was in his heart. She would probably wake soon, and he would not be there!

      ❀   ❀   ❀

Nadine opened her blue eyes drowsily, without the slightest memory of anything which had occurred, nor where she was, nor what had happened to her!

Her ears took in the drunken sounds outside, and some vague feeling of intense disgust pervaded her, that was all.

She raised herself and looked at the awful room. The sun was pouring through the gaps left by the inadequate calico curtains.

Her eyes travelled over each object, and came upon Bayard's heap of clothes and his case in the corner. It was plain to be seen that they were men's things, a silk shirt, and a grey flannel coat and trousers to match.

Nadine pressed her forehead. What could it all mean? Where was she? A feeling of fear came over her, and she clenched her hands, and in doing so touched the hairpin wedding ring!

She peered at it in surprise, then examined it closely. Yes, it was a hairpin!

What had become of her engagement ring?

She felt as though her head were bursting, it ached so, and some fleeting horror obsessed her, but she could not grasp it or remember what it was.

She felt weak and ill and terribly nervous.

Her shoulder did not hurt much except when she moved it. The pain brought back the last emotions which her conscious mind had experienced before she had fainted: agonizing fear of Bayard, and the knife.

She trembled all over, although she had no real memory of events.

She was all alone in this strange place. Where were her father and Blenkie?

She struggled to think, but it was no use.

Bayard had returned half an hour ago, and, hearing no sound in the room he had gone off to shave and bathe. He was almost ready in the general dressing-shed when he heard the drunken voices in the hall, and hastened back so as to protect her if anything should happen.

Uncle Frederick, smoking, was seated on an upturned box in the passage.

"She ain't woke," he said. "There ain't a sound."

The drunken men had reached the veranda below by this time, and Mrs. O'Hara was coming up the stairs with a tray and a jug of hot milk.

She bustled past Bayard with a knowing wink.

"Guess y're bride will want some comfort, with you out half the night, Mr. Delaval," she said as she opened the door and went into the room.

With his heart thumping with excitement and anticipation, and his clear-cut, attractive face looking radiant, Bayard followed her.

Nadine was sitting up in bed, huddled together as if cold, in her thin, transparent silk nightgown.

Her face was wan and startled, the ivory-olive

124

tone of her skin seemed greenish white, and even her usually rosy lips were pale.

When her eyes lit on Bayard, instead of the love-light that he had expected to see dawn, a look of shrinking fear came into them!

He caught his breath as if a stab went through his heart.

To Nadine, in her still-dazed consciousness, he only represented pain and a knife.

Mrs. O'Hara put the milk down on a broken chair. "Good-morning, *Mrs.* Delaval," she said. "S'pose you've not had too gorgeous a night, bless you."

"Mrs. Delaval?" Nadine felt confused. "What do you mean?"

Bayard motioned to Mrs. O'Hara to leave the room, which she did with a broad grin on her face, full of significance.

With joy quenched and his mouth stern and anxious, Bayard came and leaned on the rail at the foot of the bed.

"Did you hear what she said?" Nadine asked in a trembling voice.

She was every minute becoming more awake, and more aware of the horrible surroundings, which she now knew that she had seen before.

"Who . . . who is *Mrs.* Delaval?"

Then when she realized that a man was looking at her, she instinctively pulled up the patchwork quilt in some confusion.

Bayard felt suddenly cold and faint, his throat seemed paralyzed, and it was hard to articulate.

"Nadine! Good God! Don't you remember our wedding yesterday, at the Justice of the Peace's office?"

125

Great tears welled up in her eyes, and a blank, frightened stare grew, as though she was trying to think, and then she shook her head slowly.

What . . . what was he talking about? Memory was returning. There was something about a snake . . . but a wedding . . . ?

She looked down at the hairpin ring with a puzzled frown, and then, her nerves all torn by the strain that they had been through unknowingly, she gave way completely.

She screamed aloud, and afterwards wept bitterly, while words came brokenly.

"Oh, what terrible thing has happened? You cruel man . . . what . . . what have you done?"

Then fear shook her. She was beyond reasoning and her faculties were not all awake; it was just a sort of panic which was overcoming her.

"Papa . . . Blenkie . . . where are you?" she screamed.

It was as if the lightning had struck Bayard. All her passionate love for him, which she had showered upon him with wild abandon, had just been the effect of intoxication, then!

She was herself now, and she did not remember a thing.

The ghastly tragedy of it.

Indeed, what terrible action had he committed? He, a gentleman, had taken advantage of an unconscious girl, *because his own passion had clouded his apprehending faculties.*

Of course he ought to have known that she was irresponsible.

He had thought that the whisky had removed inhibitions and perhaps excited her but that the real Nadine was talking and acting, not that she was intoxicated and unknowing.

"My God!" he cried in his agony. "I did not understand. I thought you knew what was happening, and consented. I—I—thought you loved me! Oh, God! Forgive me, Nadine."

She sobbed on, but his voice was clearing things in her brain and linking up connections.

He controlled himself, and spoke coldly now. He must repair this hideous mistake as quickly as he could, and try to act chivalrously, like the Knight Bayard.

He did not know enough of very young girls to know that it was the shock, the dreadful room, and the loneliness which were affecting Nadine's still-unbalanced mind.

He thought that she was expressing her sane sentiments now, and that he must accept the implication of them without an argument or an attempt to change her feelings.

He was a proud man, as proud as Sir Edward in his own way, and as well as being mad with himself, he was wounded to the core.

She had evidently been playing with him from the beginning, it would seem. And he had sworn to God that he would be her only love!

What fools men were!

"Nothing has been done which cannot be undone, Miss Pelham," he said sternly. "You were bitten by a rattlesnake, and we had to stay in my shack all night, and yesterday."

His voice failed him for an instant.

"Your father would not accept my explanation, so we were married on the way back."

He looked at her once more, with agony in his grey eyes.

It seemed to him that his duty and his honour were plain before him, and in case he should weaken, if he stayed a minute more, he turned to the door.

"I will send after your father and Miss Blenkensop and hope to catch them up. Meanwhile, I will see that you are protected until you obtain your freedom. Good-bye, Miss Pelham."

He opened the door and went out.

Nadine was hardly conscious that he was gone, nor had she taken in all the meaning of what he had said.

She went on sobbing violently.

Bayard strode down the stairs, but on the veranda he staggered a little, and sat down on a bench to think.

Mrs. O'Hara saw him with the corner of her eye, as she was clearing away some breakfasts from the room inside.

He called to her.

"Go to Mrs. Delaval, please," he said shortly.

But before she could answer him, he started up, went on down the steps into the street, and walked on towards the sheriff's office.

Nadine was still sobbing, but everything that led up to the snake bite was becoming clear, and the fear of the knife and Bayard was growing dimmer.

It had never been concrete, only an impression of the last remembered thing, and now the consciousness of her love for him was filling her again.

She began to rack her brain to try and remember what had happened, but it was no use; her head felt like wool, and the only thing which would come was the tune of the "Red Sarafane."

Why should it be haunting her now?

How could it be that she did not remember being married? And as she thought of this, in spite of her sobs, she felt a little thrill. . . .

Was she really married, married to her Knight Bayard? . . .

He had been here in her room; then, again, the confusion of being in her nightgown overcame her, and she clutched at the quilt, taking her hands from her eyes.

But he had gone away, angry. She gave a wild sob.

At that moment Mrs. O'Hara opened the door.

"My, my, this will never do," she exclaimed, sitting down on the side of the bed.

"You's just worn out. Drink the milk and that will hearten you."

Nadine had all the English reserve and dislike of strangers' interference, but the woman was so kindly, and she was so very frightened and worried all by herself, because she now realized that her family must have gone.

So her first impulse, which was to request the woman to leave her, passed, and she let her pour out the milk and accepted the cup gratefully, controlling her sobs, which had now become little shuddering sighs.

"He's the dandiest man in Gold Rock, and the whole of Nevada, for that matter, your husband, Ma'am, but girls does quarrel over trifles, and that's how trouble comes."

Nadine did not answer; she just drank the milk.

"Say, you do love him, don't you, dearie? He's a real gentleman. The 'Prince' we calls him in the mining camp. I'm sure he did not mean to hurt you. You'll kiss and be friends when he comes back?"

Nadine nodded. The milk was comforting her.

"Now, if you'll take advice from an old desert woman as knows men well," Mrs. O'Hara went on, "you'll not let him see you peeved and draggled when he comes in.

"You'll get up, and look for your prettiest outfit, and you'll doll yourself up, and be all ready and waitin' to spring into his arms, the picture of happiness."

A smile gradually spread over Nadine's face, and she nodded her head again.

Mrs. O'Hara got off the bed; she felt as pleased as Punch that she had accomplished her mission.

"I'll tell you what I'll do for you, dearie," she announced with generous pride, "I'll bring you a drop of hot water to wash with."

And as Nadine began to thank her for this welcome promise, Mrs. O'Hara kissed her fat fingers to her and left the room!

Then Nadine nestled down in the clothes again for a minute and began stroking her hairpin wedding ring.

He had given her that, and she kissed it.

And the milk having restored her a little, her real feelings began strongly to reassert themselves.

"Bayard," she whispered softly, "I love you, I love you."

She was not quite sure what he had been angry about, but anyhow she would smooth it all away when he came back to her.

He had said he loved her, she remembered that in the canyon, and she was married to him, really married to him, and they would stay together for always.

How silly she had been to cry. No wonder he was cross with her, making such a scene!

What did he mean by saying nothing was done which could not be undone? But this was still too difficult for her confused mind.

Nothing was really coherent but that she adored Bayard and was married to him; and, as that funny woman had suggested, she would make herself pretty and be quite ready to spring into his arms when he returned.

But at that moment, Bayard, seated in the sheriff's office, was explaining matters to him, and the legal annulment of the marriage would be started at once.

Nadine's head began to clear when she got out of bed. And Mrs. O'Hara, true to her promise, brought up a jug of hot water and put it inside the door.

Nadine thanked her, and when the jolly woman had left the room, the picture of mining-camp life came clearly to her.

Her mind, as far as the events which had occurred after she had fainted, was practically an absolute blank.

She knew nothing of how she had tempted Bayard in the shack, nor of all the passionate love-words she had said.

She remembered that he had told her that he loved her, when the horses broke away, and she remembered that she had felt that she loved him very much in return.

131

After the snake had bitten her, the next clear thing was her agony of fear about the knife... then oblivion, until she had awakened in this horrible room!

How had it been possible that she had been *married* to Bayard without knowing it? Did snake bite take away people's memory and their ability to reason?

She could understand being in a faint and not being aware of things, but she could not understand having gone through a ceremony and then not having any recollection of it.

She knew nothing of having taken the whisky. Her mouth felt very hot and dry and her head ached; but, never having seen anyone intoxicated, and never having heard anything about such things in her quiet, stately, sheltered life, she had no clue in this.

It was all a terrible mystery!

Suspicions and doubts held her thoughts as she tried to dress. Had Mumford been right, and was Bayard not a gentleman after all?

If he had taken some advantage of her, he was simply a cad, and whether she had loved him or not, she would only hate him now!

After all, what did she really know about him? Nothing, except that he was just her ideal of a man!

And here she was dressing meekly to await his return to her! Anger blazed up again, but then a thought.... Return?

But what had he said.

She put her hand to her forehead, trying, trying to remember.

He had said, "Nothing has been done which

132

cannot be undone," and then he had spoken of her freedom!

What did that mean? Everything was a maze, and she felt as if she were going mad.

How angry and white he had looked! It was very unjust of him to be angry, because how could she possibly have understood what he was talking about?

Then she felt giddy and sick, and sat down upon the broken chair.

She was going through the most awful moments which had ever come to her in her eighteen and a half years of life!

Any girl finding herself in such a situation, in a strange, wild country, among people whom she did not know, would have been greatly disturbed, even if she knew the world and its ways.

But to an absolutely innocent and ignorant girl like Nadine, who had been sheltered and protected ever since birth, it was all terrifying.

Panic was seizing her. An unreasoning fear of Bayard, fear of everything.

But her courage came back soon, and she clenched her strong white teeth fiercely, and made herself finish dressing.

Then she began walking up and down the room, for the racking uncertainty was almost unbearable.

"The Pelhams were never cowards!" she said to herself firmly. "And I must not be!"

Half an hour passed in this cruel way. Then as she paced the floor she noticed again Bayard's bag and case and his clothes lying in a heap in the corner. They seemed to be what her eyes had first lighted on when she had awakened.

She went over to them now and stared. She remembered that silk shirt, it was the one he had worn at the mine, and there was some blood on the sleeve—her blood!

She picked the shirt up, and then a strange thing happened! The feel of it brought Bayard, her beloved, back to her; it connected some tender chord in her subconscious!

A new and passionate wave of emotion for him came over her. What if he had some explanation to make?

She was trembling all over now. And her heart began to beat very fast with excitement.

What would they say to each other when he did come? And if he had some explanation to offer ... and ... and ... she *did* stay with him ... and he was her husband ... what would it be like?

Confusion filled her, and she had a strange, weird, fluttering feeling in her heart.

Footsteps were coming up the stairs. They were heavy footsteps, though; Bayard must be still very angry. There was a knock at the door.

She went over and opened it.

A strange man stood there with a big envelope in his hand.

"Are you Mrs. Bayard Delaval, Ma'am?" he said, eyeing her curiously.

Nadine felt her voice strangled, she was so excited, so she nodded a little, consciously, and the man handed her the ominous-looking letter.

She opened it. It was a legal document bearing the sheriff's stamp. She made out that it had something to do with an application for the annulment of marriage between Bayard Delaval and Nadine Pelham, with a lot of legal terms attached.

"Mr. Delaval asked me to show you where to sign, Ma'am. I'm to act for you," the man said.

And then, by way of comforting her, he added:

"It'll only take a short time before you's free!"

The blood left Nadine's face, the shock was so great. And then all the pride in her nature came to her rescue, and she raised her curly head with the air of an empress, and looked at the man straight in the eyes.

"Very well," she said, and walked to the table.

He gave her his pen and she signed firmly in bold characters, for the first and last time, NADINE DELAVAL.

Then quite calmly she handed the paper to the man.

He thanked her and, saying he would communicate with her later, left her alone.

But when he had gone, a pathetic little figure staggered to the bed and flung itself down.

It was not whether Bayard had an explanation or not to offer, or whether or not he was guilty of some offence against her.

Fate had stepped in and parted them.

He, Bayard, had set her free! And now she knew that she loved him, good or bad, guilty or not guilty, more than anything else in the world!

She was too wretched for tears, but she covered her face with her hands, and in doing so the hairpin wedding ring scratched her.

In a sudden gust of temper she pulled it off, and with a mocking, hollow laugh she twisted it straight, and into a hairpin again, and jumping up went to the mirror and put it into her hair.

She felt that she hated all men in the world.

135

Bitterness alone filled her heart at the sorry ending to her love dream!

No one would have recognized the face which looked back at her as Nadine's; the eyes were those of a hard, cynical woman.

As she turned away there was another knock at the door.

It was Uncle Frederick, whom she did not remember seeing before.

He brought a note, and said he would call again with the motor to take her to Gold Stamp at one o'clock, but he asked now for Mr. Delaval's things.

Nadine pointed to the heap in the corner, and she controlled herself until the old man had left the room with them, then she tore open the envelope feverishly.

The letter was written upon the sheriff's paper. The writing was strong and firm.

For a moment she held her breath, and a mist seemed to be rising before her eyes. Then she looked at it.

> Gold Rock
> June 30, 1920
>
> Dear Miss Pelham,
>
> I have arranged that the ghastly mistake shall be righted as soon as possible. The Justice of the Peace who married us is a friend of mine, so that will simplify the annulment proceedings, and you will be free in a very short time.
>
> I have wired to Miss Blenkensop at Gold Stamp, and I calculate that it will reach her before the party can have left in the private car.

136

I have asked her to remain there and to meet you, and I have arranged that the old man who brings this, Frederick Binwood, will accompany you back to Gold Stamp this afternoon.

I am called away immediately to Rockers Point, where disturbances are taking place.

Mr. Arlsen, who brought the preliminary application paper for you to sign, will represent you, and send all communications to the Gold Stamp Palace Hotel.

I can only wish you all happiness in your future life, and express my sincerest regrets for having unwittingly caused you trouble in our short acquaintance.

Yours truly,
Bayard Delaval

Nadine became icy cold as she read the last words. She felt as if death were clutching at her heart. Then she sank onto the bed in passionate weeping.

❀   ❀   ❀

When Bayard had set the easy western law in motion, he rushed to find Uncle Frederick.

He explained very briefly the truth to him, that Nadine had been unconscious at the wedding, and asked him to keep guard over her until he delivered her to her own people at Gold Stamp.

So all was done and all was said, and now Bayard resolved to get on with the work which lay in front of him.

So much for romance!

Uncle Frederick stood by the car and gave him some last-minute instructions.

"Put y'r gun in y'r belt, sonnie," the old man said. "Let them see y're armed this time and mean business!"

Bayard, to please him, took the revolver from his pocket and slipped it in his belt, western fashion.

Then at the last minute he looked up at the window in the passage which led to Nadine's room.

Not with any hope of seeing her, because her windows looked out the other way, but with some uncontrollable sentiment.

He started the motor, and as he did so, for a second he caught sight of a little white face peeping suddenly from the window of the passage.

He was going so fast he was hardly even sure that it was Nadine, but instinct made him raise his cap, and there was a sardonic smile on his stern lips; then he drove like hell down the track into the wilds.

Nadine had lain on her bed for some while sobbing. In her weak state it was difficult to regain her poise.

She had heard one or two motors come and go, and with each noise she had wondered if it might be Bayard.

At last she made herself rise, pack her few things, and put on her coat and hat. Finally, desire to go out into the passage and see what was happening seized her.

She went to the window in the passage and peeped from behind the ragged curtain. It was just at the moment when Bayard put the revolver in his belt.

It was Bayard . . . her lover . . . her husband! He was going away!

138

Then in a flash the motor passed, and she saw the hard, cynical smile on his beloved face as he removed his cap.

He had seen her! And again that feeling of desolation came over her, so she had to clutch at the window frame or she would have fallen.

She had seen him from a window for the first time, her Knight Bayard! And now it was from a window that she had seen him go ... go where? ... Away, out of her life, into danger! There was a pistol in his belt. . . . And how he must hate her now to have looked at her like that!

And in Nadine's heart there was wild rebellion against fate. Here she was, going back to be caged once more!

No, that she would never endure!

She had heard much of the freedom of American women from Sadie. She would make her own life.

She knew nothing of her father having denied that he now had a daughter, and expected that Blenkie would have instructions to take her back to England to him.

She would not go! Whom, beside Sadie, did she know in America? Lady Crombie, of course! She had always been such a kind friend!

As soon as the legal formalities were over and she could leave Nevada, she would go to Lady Crombie, in Washington.

She would write at once when she got to Gold Stamp, and tell her of the injustice of everyone concerned.

Underneath there was the passionate ache for Bayard, suppressed by her hurt feelings, which encouraged the doubts and fears of what his conduct had been in the shack. Would she ever know what had happened?

The ride seemed a nightmare to her, and the heavy black clouds which had gathered in the sky seemed in tune with her thoughts.

And there in the hall of the hotel her old governess waited for her!

Nothing of interest occurred during Nadine's wait in Gold Stamp, except the hardening of her character.

She learned from Blenkie that her father had cut her off! She burnt with indignation. What had she done?

When Miss Blenkensop became aware that Nadine had been totally unconscious of everything which had occurred, the whole sympathy of the hard woman went out to her.

Blenkie believed in justice, but at the same time a fierce resentment arose in her heart against Mr. Delaval. She had no high opinion of men in the abstract, and you never could tell how foreigners would act!

But at least in obtaining the annulment he had done the only decent thing he could under the circumstances.

Blenkie's insidious contempt of the young American had its effect in keeping up Nadine's anger against him.

She had moments when the gipsy part of her nature could have killed him, and then when she was alone at night she would lie in bed and shake with dry sobs, because she knew that she loved him more than ever!

No news came to them about him except that there had been an awful row at Rockers Point (an

140

account in the local paper) and that free fighting had occurred, quelled by the cool courage of the head mining engineer of the Gold Stamp Mining Corporation, Bayard Delaval.

Nadine read the lines eagerly.

He was dear to every miner in the country, and the reporters just "ate up" any trifle about him.

How he had managed to keep the spicy tit-bit of his marriage and the annulment of it out of the papers, only his friends the sheriff and the Justice of the Peace knew!

Nadine kept to her room during most of her stay, and indeed was in bed for a whole week, recovering, on her arrival.

Sir Edward had gone straight to Canada instead of stopping in Washington. He was too upset even to see his old friends.

Lady Crombie wrote that she would be delighted to receive Nadine, and she deplored the tragic events which had taken place.

When she wrote, Nadine had told her nothing but that she had been married by mistake!

But when she left Nevada a great change had occurred in her, and not for the better, Blenkie thought. She was often sullen, and she would not stand the least authority being exercised over her.

She was bitter, and raged at fate, and her beliefs seemed to have been destroyed, and no wonder!

Bayard had been too occupied for a while to feel, but when things quieted down and he was able to return to Gold Rock, a new aspect of the affair struck him, and the first time he went out to his shack again the pain was unbearable.

Without her, life seemed a sickening blank ahead of him!

When Nadine arrived at the Crombies' house in Washington, Lady Crombie was aghast at the change in her.

A sullen, resentful look lay always deep in her blue eyes, and her timid, gentle manner had altered into one of more assurance.

The gipsy half had begun to show.

Sir Edward had refused to hear any discussion about her. He had provided her with ample money, and had told the Crombies that he did not wish to hear her name when he thanked them for receiving her.

But when Lady Crombie had a full talk with Miss Blenkensop the night she and Nadine arrived, she said to her husband, when they were alone, that Sir Edward ought to know the truth.

"It appears that Nadine was totally unconscious of the entire affair until she woke up the day after she was married! So how could anything be her fault, poor child!"

"The man is a scoundrel, then, to have taken advantage of her," Lord Crombie remarked laconically, "and it is a good thing it is all over, and that there has not been a great scandal about it."

"Yes, but," Lady Crombie protested, "that does not remove the injustice to Nadine in her father's behaviour to her. I must write him a long letter."

Lord Crombie fixed his glass in his eye and shook his head.

"Wait a week or two and see how things are going, then we can tell Ned just what we think of her."

142

Lady Crombie agreed.

"Miss Blenkensop is returning to England now that she can safely leave her charge with us. She is a good soul and in her cold way she loves the child. I wonder if Eustace's having married her friend Miss Bronson last week will annoy Nadine," she said after a pause.

"They are coming here in a fortnight, you know!"

"I don't suppose she will care in the least. She never seemed keen upon the fellow. Ned was wrong to have thought of such a marriage!"

"Everything seems to be difficult for that poor little girl. Now I want her to be happy and to forget. We must see how we can amuse her, dear."

The first time a feeling of joy had come to Nadine since her sad adventure was when, the second evening after she had arrived, Lady Crombie took her to a dance at one of the country clubs.

Her first day had been spent in buying as many new clothes as she could. And, arrayed in one of them, a frock of scarlet tulle, she looked the most exotic and exquisite flower.

Quite close to this club a fabulously rich millionaire had just finished enlarging a perfect palace for himself, bought from an impoverished southern family.

Mr. Howard B. Hopper intended to become a *grand seigneur* in every way!

As soon as Nadine came into the room with Lady Crombie, the wife of the distinguished diplomat who was in America on the special mission, Mr. Hopper experienced a thrill!

Here was the very girl who had attracted him on the ship, and whom his friend Terry Potter had

143

made such a lamentable failure over getting an introduction to!

He lost no time in being introduced.

To Nadine he appeared a rather common man, but with a very jolly manner, and his bold admiration was not displeasing to her.

It gave her a sense of her own loveliness and importance after the life, practically in hiding, which she had been living at Gold Stamp.

He danced wonderfully well, and Nadine enjoyed it. Lights and music always affected the gipsy part of her temperament, and to a connoisseur of women, as Howard B. Hopper was, that passionate, magnetic something in her was fully appreciated.

Bayard would have felt that it was a desecration for such a person even to touch her!

"I nearly went crazy on the ship because I could not get an introduction to you," Mr. Hopper told her as they went round.

"But Fate did not mean you to slip away! And now I'm not going to let any grass grow, Miss Pelham!"

"Were you on the ship?" Nadine exclaimed in real surprise.

She had never noticed him! This piqued him greatly and added to the zest of his chase.

"Sure. I had the next table to you in the restaurant. You certainly had your back to me, but I never took my eyes off that!"

Nadine laughed. She wondered if her father had noticed him.

The rest of the dance continued with remarks of the same kind, each one becoming more bold in its expression of admiration!

144

Lady Crombie had not known what the party was going to be like, and had taken Nadine there on the invitation of a friend who belonged to the diplomatic corps.

She saw in a moment that this was not the circle she would have wished Nadine to consort with, but it was too late now, as she could see that they delighted her.

"I have so enjoyed myself, dear Lady Crombie," Nadine told her as they said good-night. "I know I shall love this place and these delightful people!

"They seem to have planned lovely things for me to do for days ahead, and it is all divine!"

Lady Crombie was too wise to say anything then, but she felt annoyed with herself. It was a pity to have given Nadine a taste for the wrong sort of companions.

And as the days went on they seemed to surround her and draw her into their vortex.

She was out morning, noon, and night. For a week, the newness of everything, and the gratification of her longing for fun and life, seemed like happiness.

But with all her primitiveness Nadine was not really a frivolous being, and there grew again the ache of dissatisfaction.

She bravely tried to banish all thoughts of Bayard whenever they came to her, but she was not always successful, and there were moments when a wild feeling swamped her and made her feel that she must break away and go find him.

At all the parties which Nadine attended, Howard B. Hopper managed to be in her train, although he seldom got a chance to be alone with her.

He sent her flowers and candies, and there was no doubt of his great admiration.

Lady Crombie had given Nadine a little sitting-room for herself leading out of her bed-room, and it was generally full of Mr. Hopper's American-beauty roses.

A sort of riotous spirit seemed to be developing in the girl, and Lady Crombie felt greatly distressed.

Lord Crombie was studying their guest with his wise old eyes.

"She is really very unhappy, Viola," he said to his wife. "Do you suppose she cared deeply for that fellow out at the mine? I wish you could get the truth out of her, and then perhaps we could help in some way."

"Yes, I wish I knew." Lady Crombie sighed.

"Her mother was the most difficult problem, and the daughter looks like she's following in her footsteps!" Lord Crombie said. "Eustace and his bride will be here next week, and perhaps they will be able to throw some light upon the subject."

But Lady Crombie only sighed again.

Chapter
Six

When Bayard returned to Gold Stamp, Mrs. O'Hara told him how Nadine had admitted she loved him and how sad she was when she left.

Bayard could hardly control himself, the remorse he was suffering was so great.

How was it possible that he had been such an infernal brute, and such a fool! Of course she screamed if the last thing she could remember was his cutting her shoulder with the knife!

It was the natural reaction, and he, who had made a study of psychology ever since he had left Harvard, had not had enough sense to apply it in his own case!

He cursed himself!

The whole thing was perfectly plain. In her half-awakened state, he had but suggested terror of the knife!

The real Nadine had been the one who had pressed her lips to his in the shack!

The bitterness of his self-reproach brought scorching tears to his grey eyes, as he strode there through the gap of the tents opposite the hotel and into the desert of sand and scrub.

And now—where was she? Was her father still in the state of anger and contempt which he had been in when he left?

Who was protecting her and caring for her?

And he, Bayard Delaval, ridiculous, self-important hypocrite, imagining he was behaving as the Knight Bayard because *his vanity* was wounded, had let this innocent child go out into the world with the echo of some scandal overshadowing her.

With the scorn of her father, with a wound in her heart, with her beliefs broken, as they must be, and all because he, a grown man, had taken umbrage at her semi-conscious want of response to *himself!*

And now—was it too late? Could he repair the hideous mistake? Mr. Bronson had written several times to him, stiffly, in purely business fashion, but if he went to him and explained the whole thing, surely he would help him to get in touch with the Pelhams again?

But perhaps his brutal and shameful conduct had killed all Nadine's love for him? Perhaps it was all too late?

He would settle his affairs at the mine, and he would then go in search of Nadine, and lay his infinite shame and repentance at her feet.

But man proposes, and God (or is it woman?) disposes!

In any case, a complication at the mine kept Bayard Delaval bound to the wheel of his work for two weeks more, because so many lives depended upon him, and during this time events were moving rapidly towards culmination in the fate of Nadine!

Mr. Howard B. Hopper was not a man who hesitated in his actions. He himself was the only thing he lived for, and some subconscious sense prompted him to look after his own interests.

What he proposed to do now was to dazzle the lovely little English peach with a demonstration of the extent of his wealth, and his devotion to her.

So he decided he would give a fête in her honour which should show her that she would be taking on a man capable of the most lavish expansion.

Russian dancers, with their own orchestra, were to come from New York, and dance in the tropical late-August atmosphere, in white fur-trimmed garments, and then finish in a fall of imitation snow!

The lake was but a pond by daylight, a large artificial pond, but by night it could be made to have a vast and gorgeous allure, as of Arabian-night mystery, or a magician's sea!

Nadine heard of this wonder being prepared for her the day before Mr. Howard B. Hopper actually broached her upon the subject!

And the insidious flattery of the broadcast magnificence of it went to her head! Here was someone willing to spend fabulous sums upon her pleasure as a proof of his devotion. Someone who thought her perfect!

Nadine was quite unaccustomed to champagne, or late hours, or flattery; and the insidious combination of the three, encompassing her each day in succession, was gradually having an effect upon that part of her nature which was primitive and gipsy.

She was glorying in her conquest of the richest millionaire of the set of irresponsible young people whom she had fraternized with.

They were all talking about the wonderful fête, and Howard B. Hopper was letting her know every moment that it was being given *for her!*

Lady Crombie had written to Sir Edward Pelham, a plain statement of facts as far as she knew them.

Whatever anger he could feel towards Mr. Delaval, it was perfectly ridiculously unjust to hold any resentment against or attach any blame to Nadine!

So Lady Crombie put it to the irate parent, and because he was a gentleman and an honest man, he instantly recognized the justice of her argument, and asked himself what he had better do about the whole thing.

He remembered Nadine's face which he had seen when she was dancing with Bayard, looking up at the young man with every expression of voluptuous passion. . . .

No, he had been unjust; now he could see that quite plainly.

But the affair was finished, and the young man had behaved absolutely as a gentleman should. The moment he had realized that Nadine had been unconscious, he had set the lenient Western law in motion, and obtained an annulment of the marriage.

But perhaps he had truly loved Nadine?

Sir Edward remembered how boldly he had stood straight up and answered in the shack, and how eagerly he had desired to be the girl's husband.

150

It was not for her fortune. Sir Edward knew quite well that Bayard Delaval owned a share in the mine and must soon be a very rich man.

No, he must have *loved* Nadine!

He had been a man all through, and a gentleman. No whining, no insinuation that *anything* had been Nadine's fault. No suggestion that he had been tempted.

He had shouldered the whole business and with pride and joy taken the girl just because he loved her.

The scene in the shack? Yes, but how had *he* behaved at Prince Kurousov's party upon much less cause? ...

If Nadine was intoxicated—as Lady Crombie assured him, on the word of Miss Blenkensop, that she was—what man on earth could have resisted her blandishments?

Sir Edward suffered greatly. He had been unjust and unkind. He had insulted a gentleman who deserved every sympathy. And now what was to be done?

Nothing, for the present. Only he would certainly take Nadine back with him to England. He would apologize and ask her to forget and to forgive, and eventually, when she had had a season in London, she would meet someone suitable to her, and settle down among those of her own nation.

And he, Sir Edward Pelham, would offer a humble apology to the young mining engineer, on the soonest possible occasion, when he returned from Canada.

So he wrote to Lady Crombie, and said he understood, and would never again blame Nadine.

151

He was leaving in about ten days for a fishing trip, but would come back in the middle of September, and if she would keep his child until then, everything all round would be forgotten and forgiven.

It cost him something to write this letter, but he did not hesitate.

Lady Crombie received it the very day before Mr. Howard B. Hopper's magnificent party.

Nadine was like a person drugged during all this time.

Inside she was sad and lonely, constantly thinking of her love, for she loved Bayard Delaval truly.

And the outside self, with every gipsy instinct in the ascendant, welcomed the narcotic of pleasure and incense to her vanity in the attentions of the blatant, incredibly vulgar multi-millionaire.

Lady Crombie's uneasiness had become so great in regard to the way Nadine was drifting along that, on receipt of Sir Edward's letter, she had sent him a telegram just saying that he should come to Washington immediately before going off to his fishing trip.

In her heart she hoped that he would arrive by an afternoon train the following day, perhaps in time to use his influence with Nadine not to attend the party; Lady Crombie felt that the child would no longer pay any attention to her orders.

The wildest rumours had been circulating about the entertainment. Lady Crombie found herself in a very awkward position. Nadine was her guest.

She had originally been responsible for her meeting the set she had now become surrounded with, and she was in a touchy and excitable state— ready, so to speak, to kick over traces.

Lady Crombie felt that if she spoke to her, she might walk out of the house, and go to stay with one or another of her new friends, which would be disastrous.

At a theatre-and-supper party that evening, Howard B. Hopper asked Nadine to marry him.

Nadine laughed.

It made her nervous, but it flattered her immensely. She had now developed the art of repartee, though, and gave him no definite answer.

When she was alone in her siting-room, having said a hurried good-night to Mr. Hopper at about two in the morning, she asked herself what she should do.

It was wonderful having a proposal of marriage, and what fun to be able to do exactly what she liked for the rest of her life!

But . . . there were many buts, which she would not face. Nadine was by no means a heroine, and had now come to a stage in her life when she could very easily take the wrong turning.

Bayard had once told her that someday she might give herself a surprise, and tonight she remembered that he had said this, and she felt that it was true.

Even though their marriage had been annulled, she had always some feeling underneath that she was waiting for something else further to happen about it.

She had come to the conclusion, from things she had gathered from Blenkie, that her father had been very shocked because she was alone with Bayard for half the night, and that that was why he had either consented to or insisted upon the marriage.

She had lost the idea that Bayard was to blame.

It was all completely mysterious and she could not explain it, however she pondered over it.

He could not really have loved her, that was evident. Here was a man who did love her, and if she could not have her ideal, it was surely wiser to take what was going to give her everything else that could divert and delight her!

But Hopper...whew! That was a dreadful name, "Nadine Hopper."

"Well, I need not decide yet," she told herself at last. "But I suppose I had better take him. I wish he were not going bald; Bayard had such thick... Oh, I must not, must not, think of him!"

One of the first things she had done in Gold Stamp was to have her films developed.

It had been almost a shock to her to find that Bayard's face came out, not the squaw's, when she had snapped the photograph on the platform at Albuquerque.

She had looked at it, and kissed it, and then put it away between the leaves of the *Story of Bayard*...she must never waste a thought on either again...both had failed her lamentably.

There were no perfect knights now, and the sight of the book only hurt her. But as she reasoned with herself about Howard B. Hopper, the strongest desire came over her to look at the photograph of Bayard once more. She resisted this, and in an evil mood undressed and went to bed.

*   *   *

Nadine was very pleased with her appearance when Augustine put the finishing touches to her hair and the high *diamanté* band in the form of a tiara.

She put her cloak round her before she left her room, because she knew Lady Crombie would not approve of her garment.

She would be up dressing for dinner, she hoped, and she gave Augustine a sweet message to deliver, saying that she was so late she had to rush off without running in to see her!

Then she crept down the stairs like a mouse to the waiting automobile which Mr. Hopper had sent for her.

Just as she reached the outer hall, and the footman was opening the door for her, Lord Crombie came in. He had been detained at the conference very late.

"What a lovely lady!" he said, and bowed in a courtly way as he offered her his arm to lead her down the steps.

But there was a whimsical twinkle in his eyes which Nadine did not like; it made her very uncomfortable.

Although she wasn't very perceptive, she knew that it meant that her host found her a little ridiculous!

His manner of offering her his arm was one

he would have employed to an elderly duchess!

Her blue eyes flashed as she threw a kiss from her fingertips when the car moved off, and her red lips were pouting and there was a world of challenge in her whole expression.

"It looks as though there might be the devil to pay tonight," Lord Crombie mused as he entered the house.

A sense of rebellion was in Nadine's whole being and yet underneath it was an uncomfortable feeling that there was something that she would not face.

She was fond of the Crombies and could not force herself to be indifferent to their opinion of her.

But everything was forgotten in the rapturous greeting the host gave her on her arrival at the Hopper Palace.

"Why, this is just fine," Mr. Hopper said, and with possessive cordiality took Nadine's arm to lead her in.

When he touched her, the same queer sense of resentment came up in her, just as it had done years before, when she was a child and Prince Kurousov had picked her up in his arms.

A fierceness filled her eyes, which Mr. Howard B. Hopper found absolutely delightful.

"Good-night!" he said to himself silently. "Some girl!"

Nadine felt deliciously excited. She did not as yet take cocktails, because they made her head ache when she had tried them, and smoking made her absolutely sick.

But she meant to overcome her aversion to both things, because it was so dull to be behind the times! Only she would not make the experiment tonight, as she wanted to enjoy every moment of this wonderful show!

"We'll show them how, in your country someday!" Mr. Hopper said during the banquet. "Gee, that will make me proud when I can see 'Mrs. Howard B. Hopper, *née* Miss Nadine Pelham' in print!"

"But I have not said that I will marry you, Mr. Hopper!" Nadine answered as archly as she could. Something in her resented his tone of assurance.

He was not the least abashed.

"Well, I mean to go on asking you until you accept me. I'm like the undertaker, I'll get you in the end!"

Nadine gave a little shiver. Mr. Hopper's style of wit was not quite what she would have desired, but she must not be so critical.

*   *   *

By the time the Crombies had finished their solitary dinner and were beginning to think of bed, and to wonder if Lady Crombie's wire to their old friend had ever reached him, Sir Edward himself turned up!

He had come by the first train he was able to catch.

"Well, what is it?" he asked after they had greeted him. "About Nadine, of course!"

"Yes," said Lady Crombie rather diffidently. "The child has somehow slipped into the wrong set here, and is getting herself rather talked about ... and I ... felt I would prefer that you were on the spot, as the responsibility is too great for me."

Sir Edward paled. Was the girl's temperament going to prove a menace for all her life?

"I shall take her back to England with me at once, Viola. She must have got completely out of hand."

"My dear Ned," Lord Crombie interposed. "You will not be able to do any ordering, I fear. You may be able to coax her to return with you, but the ordeal through which she has passed has left its mark upon the child's spirit in no small degree.

"That is why she takes pleasure in these feather-brains here. It is to kill remembrance, I am sure, and not from any bad impulse."

"I will not have the Pelham named disgraced further!" And an iron look came round Sir Edward's mouth.

But Lady Crombie wondered to herself how he would be able to prevent it.

"Where is she this evening?" the troubled man asked after a little more conversation.

"As a fête given by one of the most impossible bounders in Washington. A certain Hopper, Howard B. Hopper."

"Nadine goes off without consulting you— her hosts! What can have come over the girl!" Sir Edward exclaimed.

"I feel that it is my fault," Lady Crombie interrupted. "By an unlucky chance she met all these giddy young people the first night we went out, and they have clung to her like leeches ever since, and of course they are youthful and probably amusing after her quiet life."

"I hear the bounder makes tremendous advances to Nadine," Lord Crombie said. "But I don't suppose she would think of him seriously, would she, Viola?"

"Of course not! What an absurd idea!" But Lady Crombie's voice faltered a little on the last word.

What if Nadine should be contemplating this dreadful thing?

"There seems nothing to be done tonight, and Ned must be famished."

❋   ❋   ❋

Meanwhile, the banquet at Mr. Howard B. Hopper's mansion was drawing to a close, and new enchantments would soon begin.

Nadine had had two glasses of champagne and was outwardly in the wildest spirits, but deep down in her heart there was a weight of lead.

That strange depression which seems to cause a sinking even underneath great excitement.

She felt that she was being rushed along, and that there was some awful abyss ahead, but that she must laugh and be gayer than she had ever been before.

The scarlet flush was in her olive-ivory cheeks and her eyes were bright as stars. She chaffed and fenced with her assiduous host and with all the other young men; she had never been so dazzlingly alluring.

"Some girl!" they all felt.

Mr. Hopper had grown more and more familiar, and now he called her "honey" as they danced, and "sweetie" and "cutie," which Nadine pretended not to hear.

And now the moment had come for going into the garden, where the most exciting part of the whole entertainment was to take place.

It was one of those intensely hot, still nights, August 31. The sky was inky black and far away in the distance there were faint rumbles of thunder.

But the darkness of heaven only helped to render more brilliant the effect of the myriad electric lamps which turned the lake into a sheen of silver and ruby and green and gold.

"Oh, how divine!" cried Nadine as the party came down from the terrace towards it. "You wonderful man!"

And as Howard B. Hopper rather lurched towards her, he felt that his reward would not be long delayed.

Nadine was quivering with excitement when Mr. Hopper led her down the steps to the canoe destined for them, and when she was seated she seemed the very spirit of the feast.

The lights caught her high *diamanté* tiara, making it a stream of fire, and even her mother's face had never looked more fierce and untamed.

Mr. Hopper was triumphant.

He paddled the canoe to the other end of the lake, a distance of not more than forty yards perhaps, and then let it drift.

A wonderful band, hidden beyond the trees, played inspiriting music, which mingled with the gay shrieks of the girls in the canoes and the low rumbles of thunder in the distance, which, however, seemed to be coming nearer.

An electric tension was in the air, everyone was wild, and some were intoxicated as well. Mr.

Hopper poured out champagne for Nadine and handed her the glass.

"Drink to the day when you're mine, peachy!" he said, and swallowed his down!

The strange feeling of sinking and emptiness was growing in Nadine, and she was not quite sure what was going to happen, whether she should shriek aloud with laughter, like the other girls, or faint.

So she took the glass and drank it.

"Here is to life," she said.

"And love," Mr. Hopper added, pouring out a second glass for himself.

Nadine laughed hysterically, and rocked the canoe, very nearly upsetting them!

Then from the bower at the end of the lake the Russian dancers emerged, lovely girls in pale blue velvet dresses all trimmed with white fur, and high yellow boots.

The musicians took their places on the marble steps, the other band stopped and new, wild sounds began, and the dancers stamped and cried aloud as they whirled round.

With the very first notes Nadine stiffened, and when the "Red Sarafane" wove itself into the rhythm, electric thrills ran through her and she lost all sense of time and place.

"Oh, the dear Russian music!" she cried, beating time with her fan, then starting up suddenly in the rocking canoe.

"Who'll dance with me?" she called, and with a bound she was on the frail little table which separated her from Mr. Hopper; then kicking off the dish of sandwiches, and the bottles and glasses and plates, she began to dance some steps.

The canoe rocked violently, and a loud clap of thunder drowned even the roar of applause.

Then with a wild whoop, excited beyond any consideration, Nadine made a beautiful dive into the lake, capsizing the canoe and its other occupant as she leaped!

Yells of delight greeted this feat, and she began to swim rapidly towards the steps to join the Russians, the mermaids following her, while a spotlight fixed in a tree kept a golden glitter upon her *diamanté* band!

The entire party now were shouting with frenzied glee and excitement, and as she passed the great barge, a young Russian guest dived in and followed her!

Mr. Hopper, quite unprepared for his ducking, sank, to the bottom of the lake, and swallowed muddy water before he could strike out for safety!

There was Neptune's rock not so far away, and he made for that, a spluttering, draggled, dripping object, the bald patch on his head shining white in the lights, for the immersion had swept back the carefully arranged hair.

"You return to your element, Father," he ordered Neptune, "and give me your throne!"

And when the obedient god had plunged into the water, Howard B. Hopper hung on to the rock, waving one arm excitedly as he cheered Nadine on, his words rather incoherent because of the monster pearl still in his mouth!

This was the sort of wife he wanted! Gee, she had put over a great stunt!

Meanwhile, the Russian dancers, mad with excitement, were executing marvellous steps.

The imitation snow had begun to fall in

countless flakes upon them, from a captive balloon, as Nadine, well ahead of her train of mermaids and her Russian follower, reached the steps and walked up out of the water.

Her dress, clinging enough when dry, was now but a skin over her slender body.

Her crisp, curly hair, a little disarranged by the plunge, was not, however, draggled, and the *diamanté* band had stayed firmly in its place.

With an air of supreme insolent assurance she walked up to the eager young men who had rushed from the barge to meet her.

But she waved them all aside.

"I'll only dance with him who had the pluck to follow me," she cried, and the young Russian emerging from the water now sprang to her side.

The dancing girls made way for them, the musicians banged their instruments, and amidst thunder-claps and lightning, and shrieks and shouts of joy, the pair stamped and writhed and twirled beneath the falling snow, until Nadine fell, almost exhausted, into the young man's waiting arms.

❀   ❀   ❀

It was no wonder that the papers the next day contained blazing headlines concerning this party!

"Daughter of English Baronet Plunges into Lake at 'Poppa' Hopper's Orgy!"

"Daring Dive from Canoe by English Aristocrat, Daughter of Sir Edward Pelham!" etc., etc., and others more extravagant still.

Mr. Hopper had applauded ecstatically from Neptune's rock, and then he insisted upon Nadine's

163

returning to the house and taking immediately a hot bath when at last the crazy dance ended.

But once the dance finished, all bravado had deserted Nadine, and she was glad to retire alone upstairs to the magnificent bedroom suite.

"This is for you, if I have to wait till the cows come home," Mr. Hopper told her, and then he left her.

There was an ermine cloak which he had bought, a bargain at a summer price, and had intended to give to his mistress, just before Nadine came upon the scene.

Then he changed his mind, and it had stayed in a drawer. It should be brought out now, together with a pair of his best silk pyjamas, and offered to her instead of her own dripping clothes!

So it was in this guise, her tiny feet thrust into the big slippers, and her slender body lost in the pink silk pyjamas, and swathed in the ermine cloak which had been destined for Mr. Hopper's mistress, that Nadine, daughter in that long line of Pelhams, returned to the Crombies' roof!

Mr. Hopper and a friend accompanied her, and held her between them, because the punch he had given her after her bath had made her fall off to sleep as they drove.

She awoke with a start, and was just conscious enough to be aware that it was fortunate that her latch-key had remained in her own cloak's pocket and was not at the bottom of the lake! And that no servant would see her creep up to bed.

She said good-night very quietly, too worn out to struggle when her host put his arm round her to lead her up the steps.

And at last she was alone in her room, and

soon in bed. But just before she turned out the light her eye caught the *Story of Bayard* on the table, and she burst into a passion of tears.

Oh, what would Bayard think of her, had he been there tonight!

Chapter
Seven

Nadine's awakening on the first day of September was as heavy as lead.

And just as her eyes had alighted on a man's clothes upon that other occasion in her life when a strange adventure had befallen her, so now they lit on Mr. Howard B. Hopper's pink silk pyjamas hanging over a chair!

She bounded up. Of all things, Augustine must not see these! She rolled them into a bundle and thrust them into an unused drawer in a cabinet.

Then, out of bravado, she stood up defiantly and looked at herself in the glass. Her blue eyes were haggard and her cheeks pale.

"I think I must have been crazy last night ... or tipsy!" She then moaned to herself and sprang back into bed.

She had never felt more wretched in all her life.

Augustine came in presently with a cup of tea, her face a mask.

Augustine loved her little mistress, and looked

upon all she did with a lenient eye, but she had read the papers, and, well. . . !

After all, *Mademoiselle* Pelham was an aristocrat! And *ladies* did not generally make scandals like this!

Defiance once more entered Nadine's spirit! If even her maid showed disapproval, what could she expect from the Crombies?

She put on a jaunty air, ordered her bath, and said she would have her hair done in a new way and would try on some new shoes with ridiculous heels.

Then she went into the bathroom humming a tune, until she stopped abruptly, becoming conscious that it was the "Red Sarafane"!

She got into the bath and lay there and thought.

A cynical mood came at last, and the worst side of her nature was in ascendance when she rejoined Augustine in the bedroom.

Her breakfast had come up now, and with it . . . the papers! They lay on a table beside the sofa in her sitting-room.

She had her hair done first. Then when she read the headlines, a brilliant scarlet flush came into her pale cheeks, and her eyes flashed savagely.

All trace of Pelham seemed to have left her, and Nada the Gipsy sat there crouched up in the pillows.

Nadine gave a bitter laugh, then angrily flung the journals down.

There was a knock at the door and Augustine went to answer it. It was a monster box of roses from Mr. Hopper with his card.

"Have you seen the papers? You were great

last night," was written on it. "When may I come for my answer? Telephone me . . ." And he had scribbled the number of his office.

This comforted Nadine; here was one person who would not condemn her! In the eyes of Howard B. Hopper she was "great."

The depression lifted a little. Augustine opened the huge box for her. The roses were colossal and the scent was good. Augustine now discreetly left the room.

In a minute or two Nadine picked up the papers again, and read each allusion to the party through. It did sound pretty terrible, but Mr. Hopper thought her *"great"!* She must not forget that!

While she lay there playing with a glorious rose she had pulled from the rest, Lady Crombie came into the room, carrying the journal with the most sensational account of the party.

She took in at once the situation. Defiance was written on every line of the pathetic little figure.

Tears came into Lady Crombie's kind eyes.

"She is not really bad, or vulgar, or even very fierce," she thought to herself, "which is why she would never succeed in being wicked. The timid, gentle part would come up at the wrong moment!"

"Good-morning!" Nadine said, smiling.

"Good-morning, dear. You know, your father arrived from Canada last night, while you were out. . . . I am afraid he must have seen . . . this!"

And Lady Crombie held out the paper.

Nadine went into one of her peals of laughter.

"Papa! Oh, how it must have upset the poor

169

old boy! Shan't I catch it ... dear Lady Crombie, and of course you are shocked too!"

"I am not shocked, dear ... I am only sad. All this excitement does not mean happiness."

She sat down on the end of the sofa at Nadine's feet.

A change came over the poor child, and her blue eyes grew misty.

"No, but it helps one to forget."

Lady Crombie was just going to express her sympathy and draw out the story of sorrow when Sir Edward strode in, a crumpled journal gasped in his hand.

He had meant to be tender and kind to his child, and explain everything, and ask her forgiveness for the part he had played, but when he read the scandalous paragraphs his blood had boiled with rage.

Could she not even remember that she was a lady! His own flesh and blood, disgracing the Pelham name!

It was not a misunderstanding this time; she was not the victim of a snake bite! She had deliberately gone to this impossible party, and must have completely lost her head.

But people of breeding should not lose their heads—women at least! he was obliged to add, thinking suddenly of Russia!

Surely the teaching of Miss Blenkensop, and his own share in her nature, ought to have stood for something with Nadine!

He was white with anger and disgust by the time he reached his daughter's sitting-room.

The wildest part of Nadine's nature came uppermost when she saw his face. An insolent, sneering smile grew on her lips, and her blue eyes flashed with ugly mischief.

Her father paused for a moment, horrified at her appearance and at the change in her whole personality.

Was this his daughter, his little Nadine? This ridiculous dressed-up creature! His eyes travelled from the vulgar hair-style to the more-vulgar silver shoes, with heels four inches high!

Then he said in a voice of ice:

"May I ask for an explanation of this," and he struck the newspaper in his hand.

Nadine drew herself up.

"You may ask what you please, Papa, but I need not answer if I do not want to."

She showed all her white teeth in a smile that might have been a snarl.

"How dare you disgrace the Pelham name in this way," the angry parent continued in a still colder voice than before. "You shall come straight back to England with me immediately."

She burst out laughing, a little hysterically, then flew into a violent rage.

She stamped her foot and shook her fist with passion, and suddenly the room melted before Sir Edward's vision, and Nada stood there in her gipsy dress, flying at the chief of the troop, and biting his arm.

He grew as white as death.

"How dare *you* speak to me!" Nadine shrieked. "The Pelham name! The Pelham name! Everything must be sacrificed to that! Life and love and human things . . . probably you killed my mother with your Pelham pride."

But now she had gone too far with her father;

171

it seemed as if lightning came from his eyes, and she quailed before it.

"Enough," he said with a deadly quiet voice.

Nadine turned like an animal at bay, and her eyes caught Howard B. Hopper's card on the table. She picked it up.

"Here is a name that I can do what I like with," she cried. "Hopper! It is common enough for me, and I shall take it and drag it in the mire if I wish.

"You would have married me to a namby-pamby Pelham, and then you left me to a stranger, and now I will settle my own fate, and you and your Pelham name can get out of my life."

She rushed round to the telephone, the card in her hand, while Sir Edward and Lady Crombie stood back, too horrified to speak.

"Hallo!"

Then she gave the number, and almost immediately a voice answered, and she smiled a smile of triumph, fixing her eyes on her father.

"Yes, you may come this afternoon for your answer . . . to tea . . . at five o'clock. . . . What is it to be? . . . well, can't you guess?"

Then a laugh, and then:

"You said I was *great,* you know! I like being 'great.' . . . *Au revoir!*" And she put the receiver down.

"Now," she said to her father, "now, that is done, and you can welcome your future son-in-law."

But Sir Edward only turned to the door and left the room, and Lady Crombie followed him.

And when Nadine was alone she sank upon

the sofa again and stared in front of her; her courage and her anger had both died down.

But she was in up to her neck, truly her ships were burned, and she must go on, there was no returning.

She felt too wretched and too ashamed for tears.

There was no one in the world she could turn to now who would understand or help.

❖　　❖　　❖

That afternoon Lady Crombie happened to be having several people to tea, but Nadine did not leave her room until five o'clock struck.

Howard B. Hooper arrived promptly at five o'clock and was overjoyed when Nadine said she would marry him. He at once produced an immense single-stone diamond ring and slipped it on her third finger.

"What a beautiful ring!" Nadine exclaimed.

It seemed the only thing to say.

"It's the best that money can buy!"

"It is divine!" She examined the marvellous stone with real admiration. "Thank you very much. And now I do want you to meet Papa."

And, taking his arm, Nadine led Mr. Howard B. Hopper towards the archway which opened into this smaller drawing-room.

Sir Edward and Lord Crombie were standing with their backs to the fireplace, some lady guests were seated near Lady Crombie, who was pouring out the tea, and a few young men from the Embassies were conversing with some girls.

Everyone looked up as the pair entered, and with complete assurance Mr. Hopper went over to the two elderly gentlemen, after he had cordially greeted the chilly hostess.

"Say, I'm glad to meet you," he announced to his future father-in-law, whom he slapped in a friendly way on the back. "Guess you've no objection to giving me Nadine?"

Sir Edward's glance would have cowed almost anyone else in the world, but it had not the least effect upon the millionaire, who did not perceive it.

"Mr. Hopper and I are engaged, Papa," Nadine said, stroking the huge diamond, while her eyes filled with a malicious smile. "Do congratulate us."

Sir Edward bowed.

"My daughter is free to do as she pleases," he said icily. "I am sailing for England in two weeks. My best wishes to you both."

Then he turned to a lady near him and took no further notice of either of them.

This rather dampened Nadine's triumph. She would have liked to see him angry and disturbed.

Everyone else now congratulated them, and Lord Crombie fixed his glass in his eye.

But the one thing which was concerning Nadine was how she could manoeuvre not to be alone with her fiancé before he left.

A bitter little laugh came to her lips when she remembered how she never wanted to be left alone with Eustace either.

It was grimly humorous, really. Must fiancés always be physically distasteful? It seemed so.

Howard B. Hopper was radiant. He had no misgivings.

Once the affair was accomplished fact, Lady Crombie became coldly gracious. She felt that probably Nadine would be grateful to her if she could arrange that she should have an evening away from the giddy crowd, so she said when Mr. Hopper sprawled familiarly beside her on her sofa:

"I hope you will allow us to keep Nadine at home this evening, because I want her to go to bed early. I am afraid the wetting she had last night, when the canoe upset, has quite knocked her up, and she should have a long rest."

"Why, certainly," agreed the millionaire. "Give her all the care you can, Lady Crombie. I'll be round in the morning to take her riding. I've a new mare for her to try out."

Mr. Hopper rose with his assured cordiality. He made his *adieux* to the hostess, then walked over to Sir Edward, who was again standing by the fireplace, and held out his hand.

"I'll be proud to have you for a pa-in-law," he announced, and with a familiar pat on the shoulder he wrung Sir Edward's unwilling hand.

Then, beckoning Nadine again with a crooked little finger, he made his exit, drawing her into the hall once more.

"We'll be married on September twelfth, peachy!" he said, and bent to kiss the olive-ivory face, but adroitly Nadine turned so that he only touched her hair.

Then she ran up the stairs, calling archly:

"I am going to rest now, and tomorrow I'll try the new mare."

She disappeared into the gallery above.

Mr. Hopper waved to her ecstatically and then took his departure, triumph filling every inch of him.

175

As soon as the other guests had gone, three disturbed people faced one another.

"What on earth is to be done?" Sir Edward said. "It is a pretty kettle of fish, Ned." And Lord Crombie looked at his old friend sympathetically, while Lady Crombie clasped her delicate hands.

"It is not all the poor child's fault. I am convinced that she still cares for that young man out at the mine, and all this is just bravado.

"Ah, if only he had been a gentleman!" she exclaimed. "How fortunate it would have been, because such a nature as Nadine's can only be influenced by love."

"He *was* a gentleman, Viola." Sir Edward's voice was quite low. "The affair was one unlucky series of misunderstandings, which I have only lately understood—and you really think she cares for the fellow still?"

There was a shade of hope in the tone.

"I am sure of it. She admitted to me this morning that this excitement, while it did not bring happiness, helped her to forget."

"I should prefer that she married one of her own nation. Still, Delaval was just the sort of character who would know how to deal with her, and I believe he really loved her too." Sir Edward sighed.

"How could we communicate with him?" Lady Crombie asked eagerly, her woman's heart touched by the thought of romance. "If he knew what she is thinking of doing, he might ... "

"It would be a delicate business to call him back, not knowing either of their views," Lord Crombie interrupted diplomatically. "You could probably elicit Nadine's, but it would not be easy to explain things in a letter to the young man."

"My partner Bronson is due here in the next few days, and he might be able to help," Sir Edward said.

"For the moment there seems nothing to be done." And there was a look of despair in his face. "But will you explain one thing to me, Viola? How could a girl like Nadine, who has never in her life mixed with any but gentlepeople, possibly contemplate marrying an intolerable cad like Mr. Howard B. Hopper? Women are incredible creatures."

"They want love, and if they cannot have that, they are capable of every folly," Lady Crombie answered sadly. "I will try and see what I can do with Nadine; and you, Ned, had better hasten Mr. Bronson's arrival as much as you can."

And so the three went up to dress for dinner, each feeling not very hopeful of results.

And Nadine, up in her sitting-room, had ordered a wood fire to be lit in the open grate, she felt so cold and strange; and there she stood, looking into the crackling flames, obstinate, stubborn misery lying deep in her blue eyes.

❀   ❀   ❀

Some rather belated papers came out to Rockers Point about this time, and Bayard Delaval picked one up as he was eating an early dinner in a tent hotel.

His work had been very difficult and required all his intelligence and all his wits.

He literally had not had one moment to think,

but underneath there was a new hope in his spirit: when he should be free he would go East, and never stop until he had found his darling little girl and told her everything which was in his heart, and then if she could forgive him . . .

Ah! That was too good to dwell upon—yet.

He was feeling particularly bright as he ate the simple food.

His eyes glanced idly over the printed words, for there never was anything very interesting to be found.

Suddenly a headline copied from a Washington journal caught his eye:

"Daughter of English Baronet Plunges into Lake at 'Poppa' Hopper's Orgy!" He bent forward with sudden passionate interest, and apprehension, to read the rest.

His face paled a little as he finished the last line. What could have happend to his refined, delicate little love?

Of course papers always exaggerated everything, but still, the insinuation was that the whole party had been a lawless affair and that the guests were not quite themselves.

Nadine, to be among such people, and to have plunged into a lake! And who was this Hopper? What did it all mean?

Then he got up in rage. Here he was tied to the mine, when he should be there protecting and looking after her!

What change must have occurred in her—indeed, she was in need of "a master and lots of love!"

He had several times noticed the wild streak in her. What if she had been so wounded to the

178

quick by his, Bayard's, conduct that she had grown reckless?

Oh, he could not bear it, he *must* go East at once.

He took up the paper again and noted that it was three days old, and this party must have happened the night before—four days ago.

When—when could he leave?

But it was not a question of could, he *must*. He went out of the tent rapidly. So much depended upon his full report of the new mine.

If he sat up all night he could perhaps leave in the morning. He could then be in Washington in five days, which would be the eleventh of September.

But to do this he could not waste one instant in thought; his whole mind must be concentrated upon the problems before him.

And it was here that the strong, fine character of the man showed, and the complete control he possessed over himself.

Master of his iron will, for as the hours passed he did not give way to the temptation of memory or anticipation, he just doggedly stuck to his work, all that afternoon and on through the long night, and at dawn when he was drinking strong coffee to keep his mind alert, a friend came into the shack with a telegram for him.

It had come the evening before, and had stayed in the rough post office.

He opened it indifferently, for he often got telegrams about his work.

Come immediately and join me, imperative. Chuck work. Must be here before 12th.

Elihu Bronson, Willard Hotel, Washington, D.C.

What had happened? Did the telegram concern the mine or Nadine?

In any case, he had finished his task and now there was not one moment to be lost, and even so he was not sure if he could make it before the twelfth.

In less than half an hour he was off, racing through the desert in his automobile—to find what?

* * *

Four days of the engagement had gone by, and nothing that Lady Crombie said had had the least effect upon Nadine.

She was like a block of ice generally, alternating with wild fits of gaiety.

She had turned a frozen Pelham stare upon her kind hostess, which would have done justice to her father, when that lady most tactfully tried to appeal to her heart, in a suggestion that she probably did not love Mr. Hopper but perhaps did love someone else.

"I do not understand in the least what you are talking about," the stubborn girl retorted loftily. "I am entirely satisfied with Mr. Hopper."

She could not force herself to say "Howard."

"And I am greatly looking forward to my new life, so none of you need try to dissuade me from having the smartest wedding of the year on the twelfth of this month."

"Very well, dear, there is nothing further to be done then." And Lady Crombie relapsed into si-

lence for a while, and then talked of something
else.

Eustace and Sadie had been delayed in New
York, and now they would not arrive until the day
before the wedding, when it had been arranged
that a reception should be held which should in-
clude all the diplomatic corps and every distinguished person in Washington at the time.

On the third day Mr. Bronson arrived in
Washington to await Sadie and Eustace.

He went to the Crombies' house in the afternoon and found Lady Crombie, her husband, and
Sir Edward having tea.

Nadine was out with her feather-brain friends,
as usual. Mr. Bronson had missed seeing the announcement of the engagement in the papers, as
he had been on the train, and the news of it came
as a shock to him.

"There is someone out West who will feel this
as an awful blow, Sir Edward," he said. "You know
we all misjudged that young man."

"I know it."

"Can you do nothing, Mr. Bronson, to get him
to come here in time?" Lady Crombie interrupted.
"The only thing to save the poor misguided child
is someone as strong and brave as young Lochin-
var.

"I am sure she loves Mr. Delaval, but she will
go through with this horrible marriage just out of
obstinacy unless he comes here and prevents her.
Oh, do make him, Mr. Bronson."

Her gentle voice was full of pleading. Sir
Edward and Lord Crombie did not speak, but
their looks were eloquent also with entreaty.

Mr. Bronson never wasted many words.

181

"I'll do my darnedest!" And he went at once to the writing-table and wrote a telegram to Bayard Delaval.

"If he starts straight away he'll just make it," he said. "I had a conversation with him in Gold Stamp ten days ago, and I have got the whole thing clear of what happened and why they parted."

"Please do tell us." It was Lady Crombie who spoke, but the two elderly gentlemen were equally interested.

So Mr. Bronson, when the telegram was safely dispatched, sat down with the group and began.

He told them the whole story as far as he knew it.

"It is just what I had begun to think," Sir Edward said. "It only shows how circumstantial evidence cannot always be relied on."

"Oh, the poor, poor child!" Lady Crombie sighed. "She must not be allowed to wreck her whole life. If he does not come in time, I will brave all her wrath and tell her myself, even on the wedding day."

"If trains can get him across the continent, Bayard Delaval will be here," Mr. Bronson assured them.

At that moment Nadine was having a clash of will with her fiancé.

Mr. Hopper had become very affectionate, he had slipped his arm around Nadine's waist, as they sat on the sofa, and showed every sign of demanding, and giving, further caresses.

The same strange feeling that she was betraying some trust came over Nadine. Suddenly she could see Bayard, with his clean-cut features and his proudly set head, masterful and commanding, but his eyes filled with passionate love.

Indeed, indeed he was her only love . . . and yet soon, perhaps in a few seconds, she would be obliged to give her lips, which she knew should belong to love alone . . . to . . . Mr. Hopper.

It was horrible, monstrous, and in seven days he would be her *husband*.

A queer sense of panic filled her. She bounded from the sofa.

"I am all nervy!" she exclaimed. "Howard, don't touch me, please, and take me home."

Mr. Hopper saw that she was very pale.

"Why, certainly," he agreed. "Poppa will take care of his little girl and drive her home."

Nadine felt grateful, and this gratitude helped her to strangle the emotion she was feeling, so that when they arrived at the Crombies' door, she gave him her hand with more cordiality than she had ever done before.

"I'm going straight to bed tonight," she told him. "I am very tired."

He did not try to dissuade her. He had been on the run himself ever since the happy affair had been announced, and an evening apart would not be distasteful to him, he felt.

So Nadine crept up to her room, meeting no one as she went in, and there she opened her window and looked out into the dark.

The weather had grown warm again and there was just a soft breeze which lifted the tendrils of her black hair.

"Where is he?" she whispered with a sob in her voice. "My Bayard, my knight . . ."

✿   ✿   ✿

183

The day before the wedding of Howard B. Hopper and Nadine Pelham was horribly wet. It poured, and the wind sighed, and it seemed as though summer was over.

Lady Crombie woke with a sense of foreboding and anxiety. Would Bayard Delaval arrive in time? And if he did come, could he prevent the headstrong little girl from throwing away her life?

Sir Edward Pelham woke an unhappy man. His guardianship of Nada's child had not been a success, and the present catastrophe was the result of it.

Nadine woke full of wretchedness and wild rebellion. Everyone had failed her, and she had failed herself.

Every word that Bayard had ever said to her came back to her memory. How true and fine he had always been.

She especially thought of the moment when he had told her of his ambition. How he would like to be so rich that he could be quite free to give his whole brain to something higher than making money.

She remembered his clear eyes looking ahead, and how she had thrilled with pride in him, and longed to stay by his side and help him.

What had parted them? Fate? His fault? Her fault? Alas, what a cruel mystery.

And instead of surrendering to divine emotion with the knowledge that they two together would climb a path to noble things, in the morning she would have to go away alone with Howard B. Hopper, whom she utterly despised.

Oh, she could never bear him to touch her.

Then for a few minutes she lost control of herself and ran up and down the room in terror.

But Augustine entered, with her dress for the reception, which had just arrived from New York. A wonderful thing of pearls and ermine—literally one mass of strings of pearls and white ermine!

Bayard Delaval woke in a fever of impatience, in spite of the fact that unless some accident occurred his connections were all made so that he should be in Washington by nine o'clock that evening—to find what?

Were the Pelhams leaving in the morning? Was that why Mr. Bronson had been so particular about his arriving on the eleventh?

That was it, of course; but even if it was so, he could follow them to the end of the world.

There had been no announcement of the intended Hopper wedding in the western papers, and in any case he had been too centred upon his own thoughts to have looked for anything in particular.

Once his iron will no longer imposed banishment upon all memory of Nadine, it seemed as though the floodgates of his pent-up emotions were opened, and the tide of passion swept all before it.

His whole being was submerged in it.

His thoughts never left the little olive-ivory face, and his temples throbbed with the longing for her.

A fierceness was in him. He desired to crush her in his arms, to seize her and carry her off for his very own, away from all the world. For the first time in his life he knew the whole delirium of love.

185

And so the hours passed.

There was a dinner-party before the reception. Mr. Hopper arrived in good time, just as Nadine was coming down the stairs to go into the great salon.

She made a beautiful picture as she descended the steps in her marvellous dress.

Its train of pearls bordered with wide ermine trailed behind her, and a great bunch of orchids were at her waist, while her black hair was done in an eccentric fashion, rather high, with pearl hairpins keeping it in place.

"Peachy, you're a queen," the enamoured Hopper said, passionate admiration in his dissipated eyes.

Fortunately for Nadine, servants were crossing the hall, or nothing could have kept him within the prescribed bounds.

Sir Edward had avoided meeting his future son-in-law as much as possible, and had left the lawyer to make all arrangements as to settlements.

His pride insisted upon Nadine's money being settled upon herself, and declined any provision from Mr. Hopper.

"Let him give her what he likes afterwards," Sir Edward said to Lord Crombie. "But with my consent she shall not receive a dollar from the bounder."

These days had been one continual gall to him.

When Nadine entered the salon there was a murmur of admiration, and it gave her courage.

She had been feeling that she would just have to give up and stay hiding in her room.

All the most charming people in Washington

were assembled, and Howard B. Hopper beamed with delighted triumph.

Mr. Hopper had taken two or three cocktails as he dressed for this momentous occasion, so the first glasses of champagne he drank at dinner began to affect his head.

Nadine, who sat next to him, was wise enough now in the ways of the world, and what would probably be its consequences.

A sickening sense of disgust and shame invaded her.

Here, before they had reached the entrées, the man who would be her husband in the morning was becoming intoxicated, in a company composed of the elite of cosmopolitan American society in Washington, people who did not indulge in this way, and who would have scant tolerance for anyone who did.

Suddenly she realized the vulgarity and licence of the set she had been consorting with and the strong influence they had had upon her.

She, who had never before seen or heard of people being tipsy in her short sheltered life, had now become so hardened that the sight of wildly excited girls and incoherent young men had grown not to shock her.

And after tomorrow she would not only have the disgrace to bear of seeing Howard noisy and boisterous at dinner, but she would have to go home alone afterwards, when he would probably be quite drunk.

She put down her glass without tasting it; she had become very pale.

Her fiancé, for his part, was in seventh heaven; his natural, insolent self-assurance, exaggerated by what he had imbibed, was more blatant than it had ever been before.

Nadine nearly went into a fit of hysterical laughter when she caught sight of the face of an exquisite old American lady, one of Washington's greatest hostesses, who was seated at his other side.

Disgust and contempt and freezing hauteur were stamped upon her delicate features, as Mr. Hopper made one ill-timed joke after another, and through the flowers she could see Eustace across the table.

He had arrived that afternoon with his bride ... and was there pity in his cold eyes?

This fired her. She could not bear pity, pity from Eustace!

So she controlled her anguish of shame and disgust, and deliberately drew her fiancé into conversation.

"Howard," she whispered, "promise me you will not drink anything more this evening. If you do, I'll go straight up to my room."

An ugly look came into his face, his coarse mouth set.

"Now, don't be up-stage, peachy," he retorted. "What's come to you?"

That terrible cold, empty sinking beneath the heart was growing and growing in Nadine. She felt as though she could not bear anything further.

Then, the important person who sat on her other side, fortunately engaged her in conversation.

He too felt commiseration for the poor girl, but he tried not to show it.

And so the dinner passed and the reception began.

Sadie came up to Nadine as soon as they had left the table.

She was looking radiant, and had already, with that marvellous adaptability which is one of the great qualities of American women, begun to adopt the Pelham air of dignity.

"How much more suitable to Papa she is than I am," Nadine thought instantly, and the pain grew.

Sadie was on firm ground and would be honoured and respected, and she . . . where was she drifting to?

Nadine was at breaking-point, almost. Visions of Europe came to her.

How could she ever be seen with Howard there? And New York's best would not be likely to receive him either, in spite of his dollars, since it was plain to be seen that Washington society were not accepting him graciously.

Instead of a gilded existence ahead, she would have to surmount difficulties . . . she, Nadine Pelham!

But worse, much worse than all that, was the thought that *he would be her husband.*

Ah, how much better to have stayed in the Gold Rock Hotel with Bayard, or to have lived in his shack and tried to learn to cook and keep house for him, surrounded by fond love and care, than to have luxury and disgust and misery.

The younger people had begun to dance in the large music-room, and the rest of the company filled the great hall and the galleries above.

Nadine had just been introduced by Lady Crombie to an Englishwoman who was passing, and they had walked on into a little room beyond the staircase together, while Mr. Hopper took this opportunity of going to the smoking-room to have a drink with the few men of his own set who were at the party.

Sir Edward and Lord Crombie walked apart.

"How I hope to God Delaval will arrive in time," the distracted parent said. And at that moment both men's eyes caught sight of Mr. Bronson, and yes, Bayard Delaval, coming from the entrance hall.

"If Bronson has not told him of tomorrow's wedding, don't enlighten him, Ned," Lord Crombie urged. "Let him see her first and let them both get the shock. It will be much more effective."

Sir Edward nodded and they went to meet the two men.

Bayard had not asked Mr. Bronson any questions when he saw that he did not mean to be communicative.

The cautious nature of the astute mine owner made Bayard decide not to interfere.

"I am glad you are in time, Delaval," he had said, "and I will leave it to you to grasp the situation. Now, hustle dressing!"

And they had spoken of the mine on their way to the Crombies' house.

Sir Edward stepped behind Lord Crombie after they all shook hands, and then he came forward and drew Bayard aside.

"I want to apologize to you, Mr. Delaval," he said, "for the attitude that I took up in the past. I allowed prejudice and circumstantial evidence to

190

cloud my judgement. I am truly sorry that I did you that great injustice."

"It was to your daughter you did the wrong, Sir," Bayard answered. "It is to her that the apology is due. I understand that things looked ugly to you, but I can't understand how you showed so little confidence in your own dear girl."

Sir Edward's eyes filled with pain.

"I had reason to fear the heredity in her, it had been my constant concern, and what I saw appeared the confirmation of my worst fears. But I was indeed wrong, and I am truly sorry."

"Have you explained to Nadine?"

"Alas, I have lost all influence with my daughter."

At that moment two people of the Mission passed, and stopped to talk with Sir Edward, and Bayard Delaval moved on, only concerned with finding Nadine as soon as possible.

By chance Lady Crombie was passing as he made his way through the vast throng accompanied by Mr. Bronson, and she stopped and was most gracious when Mr. Bronson introduced him.

Then she drew them tactfully towards the door of the little alcove.

There he would be sure to catch sight of Nadine, beyond, talking to the Englishwoman, she thought.

She pretended to point out some mutual friends to Mr. Bronson, so that Bayard might go on alone.

"He is perfectly charming, your young man," she exclaimed, as the tall figure moved forward. "How I do trust it will be all right!"

Bayard caught sight of Nadine before she saw him.

He had thought that he could not feel more intensely than he had already felt concerning her in his life, but the wave of emotion which swept over him surpassed anything he had ever before experienced.

He looked long and took in the dress, the jewels, and the whole allure. How infinitely changed had she become, his darling little love.

But it was his fault, and no one else's, so it would be his task to alter her again.

His eyes, burning with passionate love, were fixed upon the little face when she suddenly looked up and saw him.

She drew in her breath with a sharp hiss, and the Englishwoman, seeing that something unusual was about to occur between these two young people, walked on through into the conservatory, leaving Nadine alone.

"How do you do, Mr. Delaval?"

"How are you, Miss Pelham?"

"You . . . you've come from the mine?"

Nadine's voice was hoarse.

"Yes, I've come from the mine, and I am so awfully glad to see you again."

He took her hand now and shook it, and he held the soft fingers tight.

"Nadine! Oh, I have longed for this moment. We have so much to explain to each other. . . ."

And he bent and looked into her eyes, his own filled with fond tenderness.

Across the hall in the smoking-room, Mr. Howard B. Hopper was drinking his own health with three or four hilarious friends.

Then this immaculate fiancé came rapidly

192

back to find Nadine, and arrived on the instant that Bayard held her hand.

He was rather too drunk to take in the whole meaning of the expressions on their two faces, but he did grasp that here was a fellow turning a soft eye upon *his* property.

So he slipped his arm familiarly into Nadine's and said:

"I'm back, peachy."

Bayard's eyes flashed grey fire. Who was this drunken fool?

Nadine turned as white as her pearl dress.

"Introduce me, sweetie." Mr. Hopper hic-cupped.

"This is my fiancé ... Mr. Hopper ... Mr. Delaval," she blurted out.

Bayard's habit of self-control served him well, but the blood left his face.

"You are going to be married?" He gasped.

Nadine could not speak for a moment, then she nodded.

"Yes ... tomorow," she whispered brokenly.

Bayard was stunned.

"Allow me to congratulate you," he said with withering iciness, stepping back a pace.

Mr. Hopper grasped who he was.

"Say, we'll be husbands-in-law," he laughed thickly, enchanted at being able to get off this joke, and he came forward and thrust out his right hand, and with the other one slapped Bayard's shoulder.

Nadine's face was piteous, her strange blue eyes filled with a world of misery and rebellion and despair.

But Bayard was too stunned to be moved by their message. How dare they bring him here to learn this?

The worst part of his nature came uppermost; he bowed sarcastically and, taking Nadine's hand in mock homage, said:

"I hope you will be as happy as I had thought to make you, Miss Pelham." Then he turned upon his heel.

Bayard strode through the hall, never looking back or noticing the crowd.

He passed various old friends of his quite close, but did not even perceive them. They looked after him and wondered at his grim, set face.

Nadine, left alone with her fiancé, staggered for a second. . . .

He had returned . . . her Knight Bayard . . . returned not knowing she was going to be married . . . and he had said there were things to explain.

Oh, the agony of it! And he was more attractive than ever, and she loved him wildly, and he had gone . . . where?

She did not hear Mr. Hopper speaking to her or notice that he had put his arm round her shoulders.

Her eyes were straining not to lose sight of Bayard's tall figure disappearing in the crowd.

She took a step forward, and from there she could see that he was making for the entrance-hall.

He was going away, out of her life, and she would never see him again! All the wild passions of her nature surged up.

She flung the fat hand off her shoulder, and hissed at her fiancé, showing all her strong white teeth, and if her father had been there he would have seen the vision all over again of Nada biting her gipsy master's arm.

Howard B. Hopper stood back, completely cowed for the moment; he had never seen anything so fierce as this in his life.

"Get out of my sight," Nadine whispered hoarsely. "I want to be alone."

And she almost rushed through the crowd to the staircase, Mr. Hopper following her. She passed the couples on the landing where the stairs divided, and at last reached the gallery, and went through the velvet curtains to the corridor, where her sitting-room and bedroom were.

"Nadine! Peachy!" the perturbed fiancé called in vain.

For when she reached the sitting-room she slammed the door in his face.

He swore aloud and knocked on the panel, but the key turned in the lock, and that was all the answer he received.

Nadine, after she had locked the door, walked up and down the room.

No. No pain she had yet been made to suffer equalled the pain of this.

To have seen him once more, and to have lost him again. She would not bear it.

She stopped in her restless pacing, which suggested some wild thing resenting its cage.

Leaning against the table which held the lamp, she felt almost faint, and her eye caught sight of the *Story of Bayard,* which lay there under some other books.

She picked it up.

Her knight!

She opened the leaves and took out the snap-shot that she had taken of Bayard at Albuquerque. It was rather a bad photograph, but it was he.

She kissed it fondly and pressed it to her bare neck. Then her brain began to work.

He must be staying in Washington. Where? With friends? She began her excited pacing again. Perhaps he was at an hotel? Which one?

She rushed over to the telephone and picked up the book. Her hands were shaking so much that she could hardly hold it.

She found the number of the Shoreham but it seemed ages before the answer came.

No, there was no Mr. Delaval staying there.

She looked up the Willard. If he was at an hotel at all, he must be at one of these two. Would he have had time to have returned there, though?

Yes, it was not very far off.

At last she got the connection. Yes, the tele-phone clerk said, Mr. Delaval was staying there. No, he was not in his room.

At that very moment Bayard was taking his key from the reception clerk and going towards the lift.

"Oh, please ring again up to his apartment," Nadine cried, and the obliging girl rang and rang.

Bayard heard the last sound as he opened his door, but before he could get to the instrument the clerk had rung off and was answering Nadine from below.

"No reply from Mr. Delaval's room."

Bayard called down.

"There was someone ringing when I came in."

"Yes, but the party's gone, Mr. Delaval," came the answer, "and we don't know the number to call."

Who could be ringing him? It did not strike him that it might be Nadine. He had many friends in Washington.

He flung his hat and coat down on the bed, then put on a smoking-jacket and began rapidly to pack.

Only a few moments passed, however, before his well-trained reason commenced to reassert itself. . . .

There must have been some method in what looked like Mr. Bronson's madness.

Could it have been that he hoped that he, Bayard, would be in time to prevent this awful crime?

Nadine had not looked so very happy about it. Indeed, now that he could think more clearly, there had been anguish in her eyes.

Had he failed her again through his temper and his pride?

He stopped dead short in his folding of a coat.

The marriage had not taken place yet, and there would still be time to take her away, consenting or unconsenting, he added with clenched teeth! He would save her, save her from that ugly fate, and hold her for his own.

There was the midnight train to Wilmington, and there a licence could be obtained in an hour or so, and she should be his wife in the morning, not Hopper's.

He was himself at last, and a ruler, and he would claim the woman who was made to be his mate! Now, what would be the best way to carry out this plan?

He had been worse than a fool to go off in a rage. The reception would certainly continue for two hours longer. He would dress again, return there, find his beloved, and make her come away with him now, this very night!

He had just begun to take off his smoking-coat when there was a knock at the door.

* * *

When Nadine heard the telephone girl's final answer she dropped the instrument in despair.

Then she threw everything to the winds. She would go and find him—she would wait at the Willard until he did come in!

What did she care for anything else in the world! She rushed into her bedroom and seized a fur coat of soft dark mink, which completely enveloped her.

Her father had given it to her only that morning. She would not touch the Hopper magnificence.

She peeped cautiously into the passage. There was no one in sight. She would get away down the side staircase and out through a side door.

Round in that street the motors would be waiting. Adala Meeking's chauffeur would know her, so she could call him at once.

Mr. Hopper, fortified by a strong whisky, had come up again to wait outside Nadine's door, and he caught sight of the cloak and the back of her head going down the passage as he came through the curtains.

He rushed back. He would face her on the ground floor by going round the other way, he decided, so he hurried down the main staircase.

But a friend caught him here and there, and he did not reach the side entrance, after having secured his hat and coat, in time to circumvent Nadine.

He saw her get into Adala Meeking's motor before he could enter his own.

Where was she going? To the Meeking house? He'd know! She shouldn't put anything over on him!

So he gave orders for his Pierce-Arrow to follow the other car, and then he swore as only he could swear.

Nadine, crouching back on the cushions of her friend's coupé, only knew one thought, one wild, determined thought:

Bayard! To go to Bayard!

She had never been to an hotel alone in her life, and it was now past eleven o'clock. She was beyond timidity, though.

She walked boldly up to the desk and asked the number of Mr. Delaval's room. The clerk gave it, and she went straight to the lift, her heart beating to suffocation when she reached the suite.

There she paused for a moment, and then knocked at the door. Bayard pulled his smoking-coat on again and went and opened it.

Who could it be at this time of night?

Then he saw who it was.

"Nadine!" he cried, overcome with mad joy.

"My darling! My darling child!" And she was in his strong arms, clasped close to him.

But, just as it had been on the canyon, before his lips could meet hers, an interruption came, and this time a doubly unwelcome one, in the person of Howard B. Hopper.

Jealous rage convulsed his coarse face, but his early business training told him that the showdown had come, and that he would not emerge triumphant from the situation, so he had better make the best of it and secure what advantage he could.

Bayard held Nadine with one arm and faced this intruder fiercely.

"Well," Mr. Hopper drawled insolently, "I guess all I'll get is the ring!"

Nadine drew herself up, took the huge diamond from her finger, and handed it to him.

"Oh, I am so sorry, Mr. Hopper," she cried.

He took the ring with a sardonic smile.

"Yes, you are!" he hurled at her, and then went out, banging the door!

They were alone once more!

"Never to part any more," Bayard said, when he could speak; for a moment or so after Mr. Hopper had left them, the mad joy of holding his little sweetheart, of pressing passionate kisses upon her warm young lips, had blotted out everything.

"No, never any more," Nadine responded ecstatically. "Here I am, and here I am going to stay. I am not going back tonight, or ever again. ... I am yours."

"Honey—sweetheart—wife!" Bayard cried wildly, and strained her again to his heart.

Then they sat down on the hard sofa, still clasped close, and told each other everything, and when there was not a single shadow between them, they began to plan.

"We will go right back to your shack, and I will learn to cook and keep house for you, Bayard, and be a real miner's wife," Nadine said lovingly, rubbing her cheek up and down his coat, in the way she had done when she was unknowing, as they drove back to the Justice of the Peace, in the dawn.

And the words gave a great thrill to Bayard! Here would be a chance of testing her love, and then revelling in its glory!

It had always been a thought of his that he would not tell her that he had riches as great as anything she had known. She would come away with him thinking she was going to the hard life at the mine!

"You are not afraid of the future with me, are you, sweetheart?" he asked, but there was no anxiety in his tone.

"Afraid? Of course not! It is you who should be afraid of having such a bad cook!

"Do you think we shall have to get married again?" she went on. "I seem to have taken a horror for rings and ceremonies and things like that!"

He held her to him tenderly.

"Even hairpin rings!" And with an air of masterfulness, as though he had a right to touch his own property, he pulled one of the pearl-topped pins out of her hair.

She nestled up to him and gave him her hand. He twisted the wire up, leaving the pearl as a stone.

Nadine watched him.

He slipped the gage on the small third finger of her left hand, and she kissed it as though it were the rarest jewel!

"Are we married now?" she asked.

Her eyes intoxicated him.

His voice was a little deeper as he answered:

"No, not yet. We shan't be actually married until I take you home."

201

"Where's home?"

But she was playing with his hair now, and beginning all the maddening little love caresses which she had given him the night in the shack.

He felt that he must use all his self-control to be able to carry out the vow he had made in the Gold Rock Hotel.

Only when all circumstances were perfect would their honeymoon begin. Now they must talk sensibly, as there was very little time.

"Home is just a little old house down in Virginia, not two hundred miles from here. We will go there first, before we go back to the mine."

"Yes."

Nadine would willingly have gone to Timbuctoo had he suggested it. For her, everything he said and did was right.

The primitive gipsy part of her had found a master at last! A master whom she adored and was determined never to leave again.

"There is a place called Wilmington where you can get a licence in almost a minute. We must catch the one-o'clock express.

"We shall be there in the morning, and will be able to get married; then we'll head back here and go on to Beechwood in Virginia, my funny old bit of a barn—and there, beloved darling, we'll have the realest honeymoon two lovers ever had!

"The maples will all be turning, and the beeches too! You can't think what the colours are down there!"

Nadine's blue eyes were like liquid stars suffused with passionate love.

She never thought to ask a question as to

what she was to do about clothes to go away in! From now onward she would never have to settle anything for herself again.

Oh, the bliss of it!

"There will be no time for you to go back and change, honey," Bayard said in a minute or two, because coherent conversation was so often interrupted by caresses!

"We shall have to go straight to the station from here. What will you do about a hat? The cloak's all right, it will be fine."

"I'll think ... while you go and pay your bill and order a taxi."

Joyous anticipation was in her tone.

"Yes, and I must do some telephoning downstairs," he told her. "Now I hate to leave you even for these few minutes. If anyone comes to the door when I am away, don't open it. I will be as quick as I can."

If Nadine could have heard what the telephone messages were she would have been greatly surprised, but she was too busy arranging a head-gear to think of anything else.

When Bayard left her she began searching among his things on the dressing-table for a pair of scissors and some pins.

These found, she deliberately cut off the piece of ermine which had been on her train, and all the strings of pearls which were fastened to it spread about the floor!

Trifles like that did not trouble her!

With deft fingers she twisted the lovely white fur into a toque, then she pulled down the elaborate Italian coiffure and coiled her black curls into their own simple knot.

The cunning little hat was immensely becoming.

Then she cut off the second row of ermine; now her dress was trainless and would be entirely hidden by the coat. The second bit of fur she fastened round her bare throat.

And when the mink wrap was on, and pulled round her slender figure, nothing more attractive as a bride to go away with could have been imagined for a man!

There only remained her silver and pearl slippers with their four-inch heels, which were rather remarkable! But people did wear such odd things nowadays, so perhaps these would not be too noticeable after all!

She pranced up and down delightedly in front of the mirror.

And below, her lover was telephoning to the Crombies' house. He spoke first to Mr. Bronson.

"I don't know what you brought me here for, except to do what I have done in any case! Nadine and I are making a bolt of it to Wilmington and will be married in the morning. When we are safely off, let the family know."

Elihu Bronson gave a delighted reply.

Then Bayard asked if he could speak to Augustine, and his orders to her were precise. She was to proceed in the morning, he told her, on the train, to Beechwood, Warrington, Virginia, with Miss Pelham's things.

"Have her loveliest outfit laid out for tomorrow night for dinner. She will arrive about six in the evening and will be Mrs. Bayard Delaval by that time!"

Augustine nearly shrieked with surprise.

204

"And above all, not one word to anyone! You understand?"

The telephoning completed, a telegram was sent to a certain widowed aunt and a certain silver-haired gentleman, with the address of Beechwood, Warrington, Virginia:

> Am bringing you my bride tomorrow night. Will wire train. Make us a great reception. Love, Bayard.

Now all would be in readiness, and he would only have to keep up the bluff for eighteen hours more—and then. . . !

Well, it was just too divine to think about!

So, having paid his bill and ordered the taxi, he returned to his little girl.

Chapter Eight

A cry of surprised delight came from Bayard when he caught sight of Nadine in her travelling-outfit, and there had to be so many kisses and such delightful things said that it was a wonder that they did not miss the train.

Bayard had his own packing to do, and delicious as Nadine's help was, it did not accelerate matters!

But at last they were at the station. The hotel had sent on a porter to get their places.

A drawing-room was out of the question at the last moment like that; one upper berth, and one lower, but not under the same pair of green curtains, had been the only possible things to secure!

Nadine was convulsed with laughter about it all. So she would sleep in that way she had thought so very comic on their journey from New York to Chicago, when it was a fat motherly female who had had the berth over her, and not Bayard!

Well, never mind! It all added to the fun of the thing. She was not going to make any difficulties. She allowed herself to be conducted there by the porter, then said good-night to her beloved, and crawled into bed!

She did not dare to undress, but just lay there under her fur coat.

Oh, the joy, joy, joy of everything! And she must get accustomed to travelling with the masses, since she was only going to be a mining engineer's wife.

For of course now her father would not give her all the quantity of money she had had ever since she had been in Washington.

They would have to live on Bayard's salary, which probably would not be very much.

There was not a doubt or a fear in her heart.

The shack on the mountainside seemed, to her fond imagination, all that she could desire, since it would be his and hers alone!

No regrets for past luxury came to her, and very soon, tired out with excitement and happiness, the thick black lashes rested on her flushed cheeks and she was in the land of blissful dreams.

*　*　*

And so they were married the next morning at Wilmington, and were once more on the train on their way back to Virginia.

What fun it had all been! Bayard had purposely kept things as light and gay as possible.

He would not allow himself to be sentimental or give himself too much opportunity to make love.

All that must be for afterwards, when they had arrived safely at his home.

And so for their breakfast they had joked like two schoolchildren. Even during the ceremony they had hardly been serious. Nadine had insisted upon their using the hairpin pearl ring.

But as they came out and back into the taxi which waited for them, she whispered to her husband:

"Bayard, the first money that we can save up, you shall buy me a little narrow sapphire one, like Sadie has in diamonds. But I did not feel I would be really married to you without this dear old wire thing!"

He held her to him tightly, but he did not speak then.

He purposely did not try to engage a drawing-room for the return journey. She must think he was not rich enough.

So they went straight to the station after the wedding and in the train they sat among all the other people on the straight-up seats.

The weather had grown hot again, and Nadine was almost suffocated in the fur coat, which she did not dare to take off, for fear of showing too much of her magnificent pearl dress.

She grew very tired at last, and went to sleep up against Bayard's shoulder.

He held her with his arm, and the tenderest love filled him. Here was triumph for a man!

She was coming away with him, apparently to a life in the wilds of hardship, and she had only seemed to think it was all perfect joy!

And so the day passed.

Towards sunset they reached their destination. And then at the little station a motor was waiting for them.

"Sent by a friend of mine!" Bayard said.

All this country was so beautiful with the

turning autumn tints, and they got into the car and lay back in the comfortable seats.

The driver was a new man, and had not known Bayard before, so there was no effusive greetings as would certainly have been the case had he been one of the Beechwood old retainers.

"How divine it all is, isn't it!" Nadine exclaimed. "And don't you think perhaps as we pass through the town we had better stop and buy me a frock and some shoes, Bayard? I could not help you much in any work in this when we get to the barn."

He clasped her tight. Every proof of her love and confidence in him was making him feel more deeply.

Ah! What would it be like when he could let himself go and tell her of all the wild passion he felt!

"Oh, tomorrow will be time enough for that, honey. I want to go straight on this evening, so as to show you the view from the crest of the hill before the light goes."

It was always only to do what Bayard wanted which pleased Nadine. If he preferred her in her pearl gown for their first evening alone, that was just as it should be.

And no doubt he could lend her a pyjama-suit to sleep in!

Then she remembered with an unpleasant twinge the pink silk garments of Mr. Howard B. Hopper, and suddenly she buried her face against Bayard's shoulder.

"Oh, I have such a lot of stupid things to tell you that I did when I was unhappy," she whispered.

But he bent down and kissed her. They had now come into the beech woods skirting the little town.

"I do not want to know of them, sweetheart. Whatever you did was my fault for leaving you all alone."

"Well, there is one thing I never did, Bayard ... I never let Mr. Hopper kiss me ... only my cheek the first day when he asked me to marry him. I always felt even through everything that I only belonged to you."

"My darling, my little girl, and once I swore that I should be your only love, and that if a man could hold a woman I would hold Nadine.

"Then I let wounded vanity take you from me. But it has not been for long!"

"And I have never loved anyone else in all my life. I have never stopped loving you, and I never shall!"

❀　❀　❀

They came to the crest of the hill presently, from where Beechwood could be seen, and when they reached the curve, Bayard made the chauffeur stop the car, and he lifted Nadine down.

"I want you to come with me along the path, honey, and I will show you our home."

She clung to him, full of interest and excitement.

And when they passed beyond the turn and out of sight of the driver, Bayard picked her up and carried her, as her tiny feet in their silver and pearl slippers were hardly suited to the rough road.

He clasped her like a baby, her light weight

as nothing in his strong arms, and in a minute they reached an old fence with a tree stump beside it. He set her down on this, and stood with his arm round her as she sat there.

It was an exquisite view.

Down below was a deep valley filled with beeches, just beginning to turn towards gold, and up on the opposite hill the top of a big old rambling white southern house could be seen, nestling in what looked to English eyes to be park-like land.

But nearer the valley, and in the middle distance, a little old slave shanty jutted out, with a shingle lean-to at its side.

Bayard pointed before him with his free hand; the other was holding her to him.

"There is my home."

Nadine's eyes were fixed on the shanty, which she thought he meant.

And for one single instant she felt a faint shock, but then she put out her arms and encircled his neck.

"Bayard, I am glad it is so tiny ... I love you ... I love you ... and you must teach me how to keep it, and how to make you happy there, my darling one."

He saw in an instant her mistake. He had not meant to deceive her.

This had been the moment he had been waiting for, when he should have the joy of showing her his home, but now it was augmented a hundredfold.

Here she was willing to go and live with him, fond and loving and contented, in Uncle Ephraim's cabin—and after Pelham Court!

This was love indeed, and no man could crave for more!

He framed her little olive-ivory face in his hands and looked deep into her blue eyes. And his own filled with moisture, so great was his emotion.

"My God!" he whispered worshippingly. "Nadine—my soul."

Then their lips met in a long, long kiss of rapture.

"Come," he said a few moments after, "we must be getting on."

And he picked her up in his arms again to carry her back to the car.

But, looking over his shoulder, Nadine exclaimed:

"There's smoke coming out of the chimney, Bayard. Is someone there?"

"Yes, they will be preparing supper for us. Come along!"

And then they laughed joyously when they were in the car.

The chauffeur took them at a great speed now, and in a minute or two they seemed to be sweeping through white-painted open gates and up a gravel drive bordered by giant beech trees.

"But, Bayard, isn't he going the wrong way? ...Oh!"

For they had come round a bend and were at the front door of a great white house in the old colonial style.

And standing under the portico were a stately old lady and gentleman, and behind them a group of old servants grinning with joy.

Nadine clung to her husband timidly, overcome with the surprise.

But what a welcome they had!

And how delightful the old hall looked with its great open fireplace filled with blazing logs.

"We've had a runaway marriage, Aunt Sylvia," Bayard said, laughing joyously. "See, Nadine is still in her party clothes!"

Such delight to all concerned.

And Nadine was embraced and laughed over. Then, with Bayard's arm round her, she was taken through the hall, past the bowing, merry servants, up the broad old stairs, and to a room of chintzes and old mahogany furniture, polished for a hundred years by willing hands.

It all smelt of roses and lavender, for great bouquets of both flowers were there.

On the bed Nadine's lovely tea-dress was laid, and all her finest underthings ... and beyond, in the bathroom, she could see Augustine pouring the scent into her bath!

"Oh, Bayard, I am so happy ... so happy!" she cried tremulously. "But I would have loved you just the same had it been only the shack."

"And now we are really married," he said as he held her to his heart, with wild passion in his eyes. "I will show you how I adore you, darling little girl. How I worship your trust and belief in me—my honey—my little Queen!"